Megan felt alternately as if she was being courted by The Band and held at arm's length. It was as if they wanted to know everything about her—to capture her like a little prize—but didn't want her to know about them. What was their big secret?

Suddenly her thoughts were interrupted by a scuffle in the shadows. Through the haze, she saw it was Ethan Hayes, caught in a tight circle of Band members. Whatever they were saying to him, it was clear he was freaked out. Suddenly, he broke free and ran into the thick darkness of the night. As he disappeared into the blackness, he let out a scream that pierced the night. Everyone stood frozen.

"Shouldn't we go and try to find him?" Megan asked.

"He made the decision to leave," Shane said, ice in his voice. "So he takes his chances . . ."

the band

CARMEN ADAMS

AN AVON  FLARE BOOK

THE BAND is an original publication of Avon Books. This work has never before appeared in book form. This work is a novel. Any similarity to actual persons or events is purely coincidental.

AVON BOOKS
A division of
The Hearst Corporation
1350 Avenue of the Americas
New York, New York 10019

Copyright © 1994 by Carol Anshaw
Published by arrangement with the author
Library of Congress Catalog Card Number: 93-90900
ISBN: 0-380-77328-7
RL: 5.9

First Avon Flare Printing: May 1994

AVON FLARE TRADEMARK REG. U.S. PAT. OFF. AND IN OTHER COUNTRIES, MARCA REGISTRADA, HECHO EN U.S.A.

Printed in the U.S.A.

RA 10   9   8   7   6   5   4   3   2   1

For B.J.M. and M.K.K.

This was the hardest part—pumping up her confidence, walking up the front steps of a new school for the first time. Moving into the crush of kids pushing and laughing and play-punching and high-fiving as they careened through the last minutes of freedom before the metallic bell clanged and classes began for the day. It was here Megan had to pretend she didn't notice the others looking her over, sizing her up—new kid on the block.

She figured she at least ought to be getting good at this by now. Her family had moved five times in the years she'd been going to school. Or rather *schools*. This was her sixth. And from the looks of it, it was not going to be her favorite.

The last place they'd lived had been great—Boulder, Colorado. Megan had fallen in love with the mountains and the thin, crisp air. She was a runner, and Boulder had been a challenge to her legs and lungs. She and her best friend, Sarah, would meet in the early mornings and start back up the road behind their houses, and almost immediately they'd be into the foothills—muddy in late winter, but by the spring, technicolor with wildflowers. And higher up, the surrounding mountains capped with snow.

And then they moved. Her family had packed into their station wagon and come here, to the opposite end of the earth. Blue Mesa. A small town in the middle of the California desert. The mesa had to be somewhere outside of town because from what Megan had seen so far, this was the flattest, driest, most deadly boring place she could imagine. The town really should have been named something more appropriate. Like Last Ditch. Dry Gulch. Dead End.

The days were searingly hot with tricky, skittering winds. Nights, the temperature plummeted and the winds stopped being tricky and started getting serious—howling out of the desert, echoing the moaning of the coyotes that stood around the edges of things at night. Late one night, while she was sitting in the car waiting for her mother to buy milk at the 7-Eleven, Megan saw two yellow eyes glowing eerily in the darkness at the back of the parking lot.

Maybe living in the desert would just take getting used to, but so far it mostly felt weird, like a place you wanted to get away from, not somewhere you could get cozy and settle in. She wished her dad hadn't taken this job, dragging all of them— her and her mom and her little brother Abe—all the way out here to the Middle of Nowhere. It had to be the middle—you couldn't see Somewhere in any direction. Just more scrubland, a few Joshua trees, here and there a billboard. She looked ahead and saw two long years stuck here before she could graduate and go off to college somewhere. Somewhere *else*.

Once through the front door of the school, Megan wound her way through the halls (all school halls,

2

she was convinced, had exactly the same smell, a mix of floor wax, ammonia, sweat, and orange peels), like an explorer with a computer printout for a map, until she found her homeroom—117. She took a seat against the back wall, leaning her head against the bumpy surface of the painted cinderblock. She always sat in the back, so she could observe without being too observed in return.

The kids here seemed different from the ones in Boulder, although it would have been hard for her to say exactly how. Less fashion-oriented for one thing. Hardly anyone was wearing major label clothes. *Beverly Hills 90201* this was not. One or two of the guys had earrings and sideburns, but most of them wore regular short hair, regular Levi's. T-shirts with the sleeves rolled up, cowboy boots. The girls mostly had mall hair—short in the front and gelled, long in the back and falling scraggly around their shoulders. Tights and short skirts and long sweaters, jeans and big T-shirts. Too much makeup. Basically, they looked small town, like they had all been here their whole lives, and didn't mind.

Through the whole day, maybe three of them spoke to her. A girl in her social studies class asked Megan where she was from. She herself had only been here a year. Before that she'd lived with her father in a town called Platteville.

"It's much cooler here," she told Megan. "Lots more happening."

Megan must have looked disbelieving because the girl went on, "Of course, about the only thing happening in Platteville was the stoplight on the one corner."

"Oh," Megan said.

"Yeah. Green, yellow, red. Green, yellow, red."

"Oh. Well then, I can see why this is a big step up." Maybe if she pretended to herself that she'd just come here form Platteville, Blue Mesa would seem exciting.

At lunchtime, she went through the salad bar, then brought her tray over to a table that was sparsely populated so she wouldn't be barging into any cliques. She sat at the other end—as far away as she could get—from two totally revolting boys, the kind you could tell had been banished from every other table in the cafeteria. They were punching each other and laughing like goons and trying to push each other off their chairs. Whatever stupid thing one said, the other thought was hilarious.

"Want some snot?" one of them asked, holding out a dish of tapioca pudding toward Megan. This was the second person who spoke to her on her first day at Mojave High.

The third was later in the afternoon, in last-period music class. Megan had been playing the clarinet since she was seven, and had taken music at every one of the schools she'd gone to.

This music teacher's name was Mr. Sneed, and apparently he was late today, so everyone was just goofing. These were the sort of moments Megan dreaded on first days at a new school. At least in class you weren't expected to talk to anyone, and during change of classes, you could just look like you were in a hurry. But when there was nothing else happening, you had to sit there while everyone else hung out with friends.

4

She tried not to be obvious while she was scoping everyone out. Usually she liked the kids she met in music classes and band and orchestra practices. Maybe there were commonalities between people who made music. Under-the-surface affinities.

"You're new here, aren't you?" came a voice from behind her. She turned to find a sandy-haired guy sitting in the chair behind hers. He had a wide, friendly face with a trace of childhood freckles across his nose and cheeks. He was wearing '50s-style glasses and holding an oboe and there was a sparkling quality to his eyes that intrigued her. He was what she thought of as a "low-key hunk." Not one of those guys who burst onto every scene and dominated with his presence. He was more laid-back than that, but a hunk nonetheless. Which wasn't true of all musicians. His chest strained against the fabric of his polo shirt, and his arms had the sinewy muscles of someone who pumped a lot of iron. She tried to get her mind back on his question.

"Mmmhmm," she said. "We just moved."

"Do you hate it?"

She burst out laughing. He'd caught her so off-guard.

"Well, kind of," she admitted.

"It grows on you," he said. "I didn't think much of it when we first came here, either. But now I'm beginning to make some pretty cool friends." He nodded, as if he were convincing himself of this fact rather than just telling it to Megan.

"Kids here"—she gestured around the room—"in the school orchestra?"

"Oh, uh, no. They don't go to school here."

"I thought Mojave *was* the only school around here."

5

"Well, they don't really go to school. They're kind of beyond that."

This made Megan laugh. "Well, now that you mention it, I think *I* might be beyond school." She stroked her chin like Sherlock Holmes pondering a clue. "Now, how do I get my parents to understand that, though?"

He smiled at this, and when she introduced herself, he responded in kind.

"Toby. Toby Schaeffer. I'm a sophomore here. What about you?"

"Junior," Megan said. "I'll try not to lord it over you."

They were interrupted by the loud, insistent tapping of a baton against a music stand. Mr. Sneed had shown up while she'd been distracted and was trying to whip everybody into some kind of order. From there, he went on to organizing the orchestra, listening to the playing of new students and trying to get first, second, and third chairs established for violins and clarinets, and talking to them about the repertoire he was hoping to work up before the big Christmas concert.

When class was over, Toby seemed to be waiting around for Megan while she packed up her clarinet and sheet music. The two of them walked out together, talking about Sneed and the monster repertoire he wanted them to learn. Toby told her how the pressure really cranked up through November and December.

"They take the Christmas concert seriously around here," he said. "Practically the whole town shows up for it."

By this time, they had emerged into the oppressive heat of the desert afternoon. From the easy way he

6

was staying by her side, Megan thought he might even walk her home from school.

But then he stopped and looked toward the curb in front of the school where an old, black Camaro—in gleaming mint condition, as if it had just driven in, straight from the 1970s—sat rumbling in neutral. It was impossible to see if anyone was inside; the windows were saturated with a heavy black tint. Slowly the door on the passenger side opened and someone got out—a guy so blond and good-looking Megan had trouble getting air for a moment. His hair was pulled back in a ponytail, and he was wearing shades, but he pulled them off to make eye contact with Toby and give him a nod indicating he should get into the car. His eyes were so chillingly blue that Megan found herself riveted. He must have felt her stare because, for a brief flash, he turned ever so slightly, letting his attention slide off Toby and onto Megan.

He didn't nod or smile, or or do any of the things normal, regular people do to be polite. Instead, he looked at her as though he already knew her, as though he could see inside her, into the deepest, most unreachable part of her soul.

Megan startled herself. That wasn't how she usually thought—about souls. She felt a light shiver pass through her, lifting ever so slightly the fine hairs on her arms, then turned back to watch Toby move off toward the car. Only when he'd already gone several feet did he turn back, as though he'd just remembered they'd been talking. He raised his hand in a distracted half wave and said, "Gotta go."

And that was that. Megan stood watching as the blond guy held open the car door and Toby disappeared into the back. Then the blond got in after

7

him, and the car slowly pulled away from the curb, its ancient engine making a deep throbbing roar.

"Creepy, eh?" a raspy voice said as Megan stood watching the Camaro disappear around the corner. She looked back to see a small, wiry girl in red Levi's and a jacket with an "Elvis Lives" button over her heart. She had gelled-up hair and five earrings (maybe six; Megan didn't want to stare) around her left earlobe. Megan watched as the girl readjusted the huge stack of books and notebooks she was carrying, and stuck out a hand to shake. "Iris Wojack. I live on your block. The house down toward Sunnyside with the green garage door? I saw your moving truck and all the other day."

"Oh," Megan said, then immediately worried she wasn't sounding very friendly. "You going home now?"

"Yeah."

"Well, you want to walk together?"

"Okay." Iris shrugged as though she was completely indifferent to the idea. Now Megan felt stupid instead of rude.

They walked along for half a block or so in awkward silence. Megan was dying to ask Iris what she knew about Toby and the black car and Mr. Ice King who'd stared a hole through her. But she didn't know how to bring it all up without sounding weird herself.

Finally, Iris broke the silence, saying, "By the way, are you interested in astronomy?

"Astronomy?" Meg was taken by surprise. "What's astronomy got to do with anything?"

"Astronomy's got to do with everything!" Iris countered. "For one thing, without it, you wouldn't have a planet to stand on."

8

Megan pulled back to see if Iris was being serious. When the expression on her face said she was, Megan had to crack up.

"What's so funny?"

"Well, you do have a strong way of putting things."

"I guess I might be a little overwhelming at first. Once you get to know me, though, I probably just seem idiosyncratic."

Megan gave her a question-mark look.

"Idiosyncratic. Oddball. I'm unique. I have a lot of interests. Some I just dabble in; others are my consuming passions."

"I see."

"So. Do you want to come over some night? I can show you my telescope."

Megan considered the invitation for a moment. "Sure, I guess. Why not?"

She wondered if she should ask the question that was burning in her mind. Finally she just blurted it out. "Iris, what did you mean back there? About a creep-out? About Toby Schaeffer and whoever was in the black car?"

"Oh, just that he's their latest victim. He ought to be careful. It's a slippery slope. Once you're in with them, you've basically disappeared. And you *don't* come back."

"What do you mean?"

"Well, look at Jenny Gonzales. Used to be a Coyote cheerleader. President of Honor Society when she was a junior. This year she dresses like Darth Vadar and spends her spare time riding around in that stealth bomber you just saw inhale Toby. I mean, Jenny used to be a friend of mine. Now when I call, I get her machine. And she doesn't return my messages."

"But who's this sinister 'they' you're talking about? Who's inside the black car?"

"Oh," Iris said. "I thought you knew. I thought everybody knew. The Band, of course."

"The Band?"

"Keep an eye out. You won't be able to help noticing them. Basically, they own the night around here. At the drive-in, the Tumbleweed, they dominate the parking lot. Just look for a covey of black cars. And at the mall, they go to the movies and sit together, or—this is creepier yet—with spaces between them for their new recruits. Toby's just the latest."

"Who was the blond guy?"

"Ah. Shane Conroy. Leader of the pack. Did you catch his eyes? It's like they've got magnets inside. Don't let them suck you in."

Megan laughed, then felt a small hand on her forearm, forcing her to turn to see Iris looking her hard in the eye.

"I'm not kidding. If there's one piece of advice I give you coming into this town, it's to steer totally clear of The Band."

"But what are they up to that you're so worried about? And why are they called The Band?"

Iris was shutting down, though, her interest shifting to something else. "You don't need me to tell you everything. You'll find out more on your own. Just make sure you find out from a safe distance. Okay?"

"Yeah. Okay." Megan said, only half-hearing. She was already drifting off into her own thoughts. Scary thoughts, but kind of exciting at the same time. Blond, blue-eyed thoughts. Racing black car thoughts. Suddenly Blue Mesa was beginning to seem like it might *not* be the dullest place on earth.

Megan spread peanut butter on a slice of bread, then cut the slice diagonally, put it on a plate, and set the plate down on the table where her little brother Abe was waiting.

"Okay," she said, humoring him. "Not a sandwich." At three, Abe—who had been a gurgling, totally easygoing baby—suddenly had very persnickety ideas about how things should be. He wouldn't eat broccoli or egg whites or sandwiches if they were put together. You couldn't touch his sock monkey or his Ninja Turtles, and he didn't like anyone to make his bed; he wanted it to stay rumpled. As she set his plate down, Megan stuck her tongue out at him to show what she thought of his little rules, but he just smiled angelically and began smacking on the first piece of bread.

Mostly she just let Abe have his way. Otherwise he'd throw a tantrum, or start crying and not stop, and her life as a baby-sitter would turn into instant hell. She had to take care of him every day between the time she got home from school and took over from his real baby-sitter, Mrs. Hodges, and the time when her dad got home from work, around five-thirty. So, this meant about two and a half hours that could be spent with a happy Abe, or one who was wailing and turning purple. Which was why she let him have his way.

As she sat down next to him and pulled out her new schoolbooks to see how hard her classes were going to be, she heard her dad's car pull up in the driveway.

"Daddydaddydaddy!" Abe started chanting. He was home all day and so everyone else's comings and goings were a big deal to him. And, although she wouldn't be caught dead chanting, Megan was a little relieved herself that their dad was home. She'd been thinking about The Band since she got home. Today had been so weird.

Actually, just being sixteen was turning out to be pretty weird. One minute Megan felt free and happy to be more on her own now, being nearly an adult. Then all of a sudden she'd collapse in on herself like an umbrella, and be slobberingly grateful that her parents were around to protect her. But from what? Granted the incident with Toby had been peculiar, but it really had nothing to do with her. It was more like something she'd watched from a distance or on TV, vaguely creepy, yet fascinating. Why then, now that she was safe and sound at home, was she suddenly weirded out about it? Why was she so glad to see her father come through the kitchen door carrying his beat-up igloo lunch cooler, the visor of his old, dusty baseball cap tugged down over his sleepy eyes? She didn't really understand these swooping fluctuations of emotion she'd been experiencing lately. All she knew was that right now, at this precise moment, she wanted to feel everything go back to familiar and

12

regular, the way it had been before today, before they moved here.

"So," her father said, setting down the cooler and coming over to give both her and Abe hugs, "how's the new school?"

"Oh, okay," Megan lied. Whatever it was, "okay" was definitely not the word for it. But there was no point in letting her dad know that. She didn't want him to feel bad about bringing them all here to Blue Mesa. He needed the work and the family needed the money; he was just trying to be a good parental unit. So she'd skip telling him about The Band.

And doubly skip telling her mom, who was a total worrywart. *Everything* worried her. And being a worried person made her an overconcerned mother. Back in Boulder, she used to bundle Abe up against the cold so much he could barely move in all his layers and snowsuit and ski gloves. Once when Megan was only going downstairs to get a Coke, her mother called after her, "Be safe."

The rest of the family had learned to coddle her a little, especially to soft-pedal any crisis that came up. If the basement flooded, they described it to her as "slightly damp." Once, when they were in the car and her dad was driving and hit a patch of ice that nearly took their car off the road, he said, "I think we're going to glide a little here." So there was *no* way Megan could tell her mother about the strange goings on at school.

And not telling her would be easy. Her mom wouldn't be home until after Megan was in bed. She was a nurse and the only shift she'd been able to get at the local hospital—Blue Mesa General—was "PM's," three in the afternoon until eleven at night. With all the crazy, overlapping shifts her parents worked,

13

Megan wound up with quite a bit of freedom and independence. Her mom and dad were so busy working and making sure Abe was taken care of, and there were groceries for dinner and everyone had clean underwear that Megan's whereabouts often got lost in the shuffle. Which was sometimes very helpful.

"I met someone from the 'hood," she told her dad as they fixed dinner together after he'd showered and read the paper at the kitchen table. Tonight they were making tacos, one of their joint specialties. Megan's job was to cut up the lettuce and tomatoes and shred the cheese while her father cooked the ground beef and refried beans. "Iris. She's interested in astronomy."

"That sounds okay," her dad said. "Better than if she was interested in armed robbery."

"She might be interested in that, too. I think she might be interested in everything. I think she's a brain."

"Maybe she'll rub off on you. Bring those grades up a little." This was a sore point between Megan and her parents. They thought she could do better in school than she did. She probably could. But as hard as she resolved (usually right after she got her report card) to focus and pay better attention, she always found her thoughts in class drifting off to more interesting things. Fantasies of fame (fans besieging her, kidding around with David Letterman when he had her on his show). World travel. The clothes she'd buy if she had a million dollars.

After dinner, while Megan's dad was putting Abe to bed and she was doing the dishes, the phone rang. She picked up the receiver on the kitchen wall phone.

"Megan?" The voice was a husky whisper, no one she knew. It could be a friend fooling around, but she didn't really have any friends here, at least not unless you counted Iris, who seemed way too overscheduled for phone pranks.

"Yes?"

"It's the Welcome Wagon. We just want you to get off to a good start here. We don't want you starting off on the wrong foot. Hanging out with dweebs like Iris Wojack. People who have big mouths and don't really know what they're talking about."

"Yeah, thanks for the advice," Megan said sarcastically. "Now who is this?" Although she couldn't be positive, she was fairly certain the voice on the other end of the line was male.

"Your new friends."

"Right again. So if you're my friends, how come I don't know you?"

"Oh, you will, Megan. Soon. Very soon. We'll be sending an emissary."

"I'm thrilled," Megan said, laying as much sarcasm as possible on the sentence, even though she was actually intrigued, and even a little flattered that someone was so interested in her.

There was nothing coming from the other end except a short space of silence, then a neat click. Megan stood at the phone with the receiver still in her hand for several moments before she replaced it. It almost felt as if it were vibrating. She was both excited by the call and frightened at the same time. Who was after her, and why? What did they want with her?

She sat down at the kitchen table for a few minutes, holding the towel she'd been using to dry the dishes—folding it, opening it, refolding it. Then she leapt up, pulled on her jacket, and headed out the door.

"I'm going to Iris's," she shouted up the stairs to her dad. "I need to get a homework assignment from her."

When she got to the low stucco house—almost a duplicate of Megan's house except it was tan instead of terra-cotta—she rang the bell, and a boy answered who looked like an older clone of Iris, with the same thick-glasses, skinny, science-nerd look.

"Uh, I'm Megan from across the street. Is Iris here?"

"Up on the roof," he said. "Communing with the universe."

Megan nodded and headed where the guy—he had to be Iris's brother, one of the four she said she had—pointed her, up the stairs.

After calling out "Iris!" a couple of times, Megan found the folding stairs to the roof and followed them up. When she climbed through, she saw Iris at the far end with her telescope pointed toward the night sky, which was cloudless and alive with stars.

"I forgot you were coming over," she said distractedly.

"I wasn't," Megan said, sitting down on the cool tarred surface. "But something just happened and I need to talk with you."

"Shoot," Iris said, pulling herself away from the telescope, putting her glasses back on, and sitting next to Megan.

Megan told Iris about the mystery call, then, when she was done, added, "I think it was The Band."

"Brilliant, Sherlock," Iris said.

"But why?"

"I told you, they're scouting for new talent."

"But what do they want from me?"

"To join up with them. Give up the life you have now and turn yourself over to them."

"You make them sound like some sort of cult."

Iris didn't say anything in response.

"Why are they called The Band?"

Iris shook her head. "Who knows? They don't play instruments, or anything like that. Or march at half-time at the Coyote games. Basically they just seem to hang out together, wear great clothes, and drive great cars—always black. It's their signature color."

"How many of them are there? All I've really seen is the blond guy."

"Shane Conroy. He and Laura Hunter seem to be the leaders of the pack."

"Do they go together?"

"Hard to tell. Hard to tell anything like that as far as The Band is concerned. It's like they're *all* all over each other, but it doesn't really seem like anyone is involved with anyone else. I mean, I don't think they break down into couples. It's more like they're this big, symbiotic organism. They all inhale and exhale with the same breath.

"Shane and Laura look a little alike, but not like brother and sister so much as intergalactic visitors from the same planet. She's tall and blond just like him, with those same pale blue laser eyes. And then there's Joey Santino. I'll point him out when we see him. Short and dark, with curly hair. Real nervous. You know, edgy. and there's James Frederick. He's thin and pale and creepy-looking. The cool and aloof type. I mean, I don't think anyone has ever called him 'Jim,' if you know what I mean. And who else?—oh, sure. Natalie Eng. You can't miss her. Tiny. Weighs about a pound. Short black hair, very serious. Like, I can't imagine her ever smiling."

Iris stopped a moment to think.

"I think that's all, of the core group anyway. Not counting their protégés of the moment. Which should *not* include you, by the way, in case I haven't made my point."

"Don't be silly," Megan said, tossing her long, crimped hair back over her shoulders. "I just want to know what's going on around this town. I'm just curious."

"Sometimes curiosity can be dangerous," Iris said, pulling her glasses off and looking back into her telescope. "Look what it did to the cat."

Megan slept restlessly, her dreams filled with The Band. They were playing woodwinds and brass instruments in the school orchestra, sitting behind her, playing a haunting song that ran underneath and opposite what the rest of the kids were playing. In the dream, she resisted, but eventually couldn't help it, and started playing along with them.

When she awoke, she was sweating, and had tangled the sheet around herself, as though a fever—not just a dream—had passed through her during the night. It was not quite dawn yet. She figured she probably wasn't going to get any more sleep, so she crawled out of bed and slipped into her shorts and cut-off sweatshirt and running shoes. One thing Blue Mesa had over Boulder was that it was flat, which made running easier—if she got out early enough in the morning, before the heat of the day started.

She did her stretches, put on her Walkman, and headed out toward the highway. She could just see the sun coming up over the flat desert horizon. A couple of Joshua trees stood in silhouette against the narrow band of orange pushing up against the navy blue of the predawn sky.

Because she had the Walkman on, she was sort of sealed into a bubble with REM, so she didn't hear anything unusual. Her first perception that something was off was a *feeling*, a tremor in the ground beneath her feet. She looked up and behind her, but couldn't see any source for the vibration. Then, just as she was beginning to get nervous that this must be one of the earthquakes she'd dreaded ever since she'd moved from Boulder, the sky darkened and there was a rush like wind, but cold and damp. Not anything like the hot, dry winds out here in the desert.

This moving air had none of the usual currents of wind, either. It felt more like the flapping of wings. It was as though she was in the shadow of some huge, primitive winged creature.

And then these sensations suddenly changed form and the tremor turned into a rumble of pavement; the beating wings turned into a huge, crushing rush of air as a black Camaro sped by, slipping over onto the shoulder as it passed her, coming close enough that she could feel metal graze the hair on her arms.

"What the . . . ?" she shouted and raised her fist, but by then she was quickly being left in a cloud of exhaust.

She stopped running and looked down at herself. She had sweated through her clothing and was shaking as though she was shivering with cold. She ripped off her earphones and could hear the other stereo—the one in the car—playing "American Pie," the old Don McLean song. She could smell exhaust and the smoke of a night's worth of cigarettes. As she stood watching the car disappear in a quick dip over the horizon, she understood she had been paid a visit by The Band. And that they were on their way home for the night.

Mojave High was turning out to surprise Megan. It was a pretty cool school in spite of being out in the sticks. Her schedule included a French class with interactive computers, a cooking class that had more boys in it than girls, and social studies, which was really more like a news show. Ms. Foster, the teacher, was hip; she used TV and magazines for assignments instead of just some textbook. It was still school, but Megan found herself drifting off less than usual. Maybe she'd even become a good student here! She'd had this fantasy before, though, and it hadn't come true.

She was so absorbed by all this that she could almost push The Band from her mind. Almost. Every day that week during change of classes and lunch period and outside before and after school, she looked around for Shane Conroy, the blond guy she'd seen get out of what she now thought of as the "Bandmobile," and for anyone else who matched Iris's descriptions. But she never spotted anyone like this around school. Toby had said his friends were "beyond school," whatever that meant. Maybe they'd graduated. But then why were they still hanging together, cruising the drive-in and cozying up to high school kids? Why didn't they have lives of their own? Jobs?

Toby was back to his old, friendly self in music class. He never mentioned having left so abruptly after school that day. On Thursday, he was waiting for her in the hall after class.

"I was wondering if you'd consider lowering yourself to go to the movies Saturday with a sophomore?"

"Sure," Megan teased. "Just wear shades so no one sees who I'm with."

She'd had a sort of boyfriend in Boulder—Josh—but that romance had mostly amounted to Megan enjoying how much he liked her. She'd been much less sure how she felt about him. Lukewarm, she guessed. There hadn't been any tragic ending when she'd moved. They just said they'd write. And he had, right away. She still hadn't answered his letter, though.

Toby was different. She liked him a lot, right off the bat. He was sort of shy, but just enough that it added to his cuteness. She also liked his sense of humor, and the way his hair fell over his eyes in that big wave.

"My sister did this with a perm kit," he confided in her when they were coming out of the movie theater at the mall. The confession made him seem even sweeter. She'd never known a guy who admitted to fooling around with his hair, although of course she knew lots of them must.

He teased her about being a year older than he was, asked what was her "mature" opinion of the movie—the latest Arnold Schwarzenegger epic.

"Well, as a film critic, I give it two biceps up," she said, and loved how easy it was to make him laugh. Easy to be with him in every way. When he'd put his arm around her in the show and pulled her toward him during a scary part—"Protect me, Megan!" he'd whispered—it had felt wonderful, and just right.

As they walked out of the theater into the mall, a rush of kids appeared from nowhere, brushing past them, going into the theater. Suddenly they started to circle Megan and Toby like a swarm of birds from a horror movie.

Megan saw them in quick, fragmented takes. They all seemed to be dressed in black. Black jeans and T-shirts and jean jackets. A black dress on the Asian girl among them. The tall, cool blonde girl with several earrings in one ear, none in the other. A tiny black tattoo on the back of the hand of one of the guys, along the base of his thumb. It looked like a tiny dagger. They all seemed to have the same eyes, even though, when she looked closer, they were all different colors. Or maybe it was the same gaze, looking off into the middle distance as if what was really important to them was happening somewhere else.

"Hey, Toby," the blond guy said. Megan recognized him instantly. "Stepping out on us?"

"Hey, guys," Toby said, suddenly shy.

"Yeah, Tobes," a stocky, dark-haired guy said. "We get lonesome without you."

"It's just not the same," said another guy—tall, thin, pale.

"Aren't you going to introduce us to your girl-friend?" the small Asian girl said.

"Oh, yeah, sure." He made introductions all around. Shane Conroy. Laura Hunter. Joey Santino. Natalie Eng. James Frederick. They were all there, all the names Iris had mentioned. All the descriptions perfect. She was finally meeting The Band, although clearly she already knew them and they knew her, so it was very strange.

She said hi to each of them in turn and looked them over while she felt their eyes inspecting her with subtle, sidelong glances. They swooshed around her until she couldn't really separate them one from other; they blurred into one entity with several voices.

"Hey Megan, we've been wanting to meet you."

"Yeah, the coolest new girl in town."

"We've had our eye on you for a while."

"We pay attention."

"But," Shane said, stepping forward out of the group, "you two are on a date. We don't want to horn in."

"Oh, that's . . ." Megan started to say "okay," but before she could get out the whole sentence, as instantly as The Band had appeared, they were gone again with a small flurry of "see yous." And she and Toby were once again alone.

"Were those the same friends who came by to pick you up after school the other day?" she asked innocently.

"Oh . . . uh . . . yeah," he said, sounding a little rattled.

"I never see them around, except when I'm with you," Megan said, not mentioning her early-morning brush with The Band. She was trying to pry open the lid on whatever was going on here. "You said they didn't go to school. Did you mean they've already graduated?"

"Uh, I suppose so."

"But they're out of school is what you meant? They have jobs?"

"They're kind of . . . well, different. The truth is I don't really know where they came from. They weren't here and then all of a sudden last year, they were. And they were the coolest thing to hit this town in . . . well, in forever."

Megan found herself smiling shyly. "I have to admit I've been intrigued by them myself. Ever since I saw them pick you up from school that day."

"They're interested in you, too," he said.

"I gather. But why?"

"Oh, they have a way of, well they call it 'spotting talent.' They always have an eye out for someone who might be an interesting addition to the circle. Someone who's a little out of the ordinary."

"Uh, how do you mean that?" Megan said. By now they were out in the parking lot. Megan pulled on her sweatshirt. After a scorching day, the desert night had pulled itself inside out; it was chilling outside, and dead black beyond the bright lighting that bathed the parking lot. "How am I out of the ordinary?"

"Oh," he said and smiled. "Do you have about an hour while I list all the ways in which you are a most uncommon girl?"

"Uncommon good or uncommon odd?"

He pulled her toward him. "I'd say a little of both. But I like both sides. And I think The Band does, too. You really ought to get to know them better."

"I don't know," she said. "In a way they scare me."

"They did me at first, too. Until I got to know them." He stopped walking for a moment and jumped around so he was facing her. He put his hands on her shoulders. "Hey, would I get you into something bad or dangerous?"

She had to smile. "I know you wouldn't."

25

"Okay. So you can meet them and see if you like them. But all that can wait, and there's one thing that can't."

"What?"

"I'm starving. We have to get some pizza. Emergency pizza."

Megan laughed. "All right! Let's get in the pizza ambulance then," she said, opening the door to his car.

On Monday, Megan was coming out of the drugstore in town, going through the bag of stuff she'd just bought. Makeup. Green eye shadow and pale tan-peach lipstick. She'd seen this combination on a model in *Glamour* and thought it might work for her.

She thought about her looks in spurts. That is, she didn't think about them for long stretches of time, just accepted that she was an average-looking girl with average brown hair and an average face. She wouldn't stop a clock, but on the other hand she wasn't any supermodel either.

And then there were times when she suddenly hated her long, curly hair, or thought her nose was too thin and pointy. And then there were other times when she all of a sudden noticed her eyes and thought they really were an exceptional shade of green, and her skin was much smoother than other girls' and wasn't she lucky to have all this natural curl on her side. These moments of confidence were when she wound up in some drugstore, dropping a chunk of cash on makeup or hair conditioners or a special diffuser for curly hair, as if these products were going to transform her from a nice, average-looking person into a beauty.

At first she didn't see a car pull up to the curb directly in her path, blocking her way across the street. When she did look up, she saw it was a gleaming, black Corvette. A classic from more than twenty years ago, she'd guess. A power window glided down and inside was Laura Hunter; Megan recognized her from the show the other night. Just sitting there in a black sleeveless T-shirt and ripped-to-shreds jeans, pulling her long, straight blonde hair off the back of her neck, she gave off more confidence than Megan had ever seen in anyone who wasn't a major movie or rock star.

But why was she stopping? Megan wondered; then, instantly, she knew. Laura was the emissary.

Laura leaned across the seats to say hi, and smile in a way that showed her white teeth perfectly against her olive skin. "I saw you coming out of the drugstore and said to myself, 'Toby's right.' "

"Uh, about what?"

"Oh, he's always talking about you. . . ."

"He is?" Megan thought she'd just play it cool and see what happened.

"Yeah. He thinks you're the hottest thing to hit Blue Mesa since the Santa Anas."

"Hunh?"

The girl laughed. "You must not be from down this way. The Santa Anas are these hot, dry winds we get blowing through here from time to time, riling everybody up."

"That makes me sound a lot more glamorous than I feel," Megan said. And it didn't sound like anything Toby would say. More like what Laura would say to flatter Megan. "Of course now that I've got all this new eye makeup"—Megan held up the bag—"I'll

27

be stopping everyone in their tracks." She paused a moment, then added, "Yeah, *right*" to show she was being sarcastic.

Laura smiled warmly, as though the two of them were longtime friends, perfectly tuned to each other's sense of humor, with a thousand private jokes between them.

"You need a lift?" she asked, opening the passenger door with a foot stretched across the front seat.

"Oh, no, that's okay, I'm just on my way home. I can walk."

"Oh, why don't you hop in anyway," Laura said. "We can take the long way around and talk a little. Get to know each other a little better. I mean, you know—any friend of Toby's . . ."

Megan shrugged as she thought, *Why not?* and opened the low door and slid into the buttery leather passenger seat. Laura gunned the engine impressively before whooshing them away from the curb. As Megan was tugging her seat belt around herself, she noticed Laura wasn't wearing one. Megan was pretty much a fanatic on the the subject of seat belts. Her favorite cousin Sherry had her life saved by wearing one in a terrible accident a couple of years back. They said she would definitely have died if she hadn't been wearing it.

"Hey, you forgot to put your seat belt on," Megan tried with Laura now.

Something about this struck Laura as wonderfully funny. She laughed again in that same, conspiratorial way.

"Oh, don't worry. I have a special dispensation from seat belts," she said cryptically, then reached into the glove compartment and pulled out a stack of CDs. She picked an old Rolling Stones album and slid the disc into the player. Mick Jagger and a throbbing bass line came up and surrounded them.

"We like the old songs the best," Laura said, not identifying the "we" in this statement, as though assuming Megan knew exactly whom she was referring to. Which she did.

They cruised past Adobe Ridge, the housing development where Megan lived, and instead of turning in, just kept heading out toward the desert. Megan was about to say something about this, then thought, *Who cares?* She was having fun, she felt free. She was even—what with having met Toby and now Laura— beginning to think living here in Blue Mesa might not be so dull after all.

"Speaking of which," Laura said, as if reading her thoughts. "I'm going to take you by our beloved town's namesake." Within a few minutes, it was there off to their left—a rock formation that rose like a birthday cake out of the sand. In this slanting afternoon light, it took on a dusty blue color. Laura pulled off the highway and fishtailed to a stop. "Nice, eh?"

"Wow," Megan said. It really was an impressive sight.

"The Native Americans who used to live around here used it for their rituals and celebrations. Now we use it for our parties—and for our ceremonies."

Megan wanted to ask, *What* ceremonies? But somehow she knew that would be totally uncool. Laura was clearly letting her in. Megan would just have to let her choose the pace.

"Toby says you come from Boulder," Laura said when they'd turned around and gotten back on the road toward town. "Colorado. Wow. What's it like there?"

Megan tried to describe it as best she could—mostly in terms of how different it was from here. Green and blue and high and cool.

"You make it sound great."

"You should go there sometime," Megan said.

"Oh, yeah. Well, I'm sort of tied to this place. You know, 'Home is where the heart is' and all."

Odd thing to say for someone who'd only been here herself since last year. But Megan didn't want to seem contentious and so she just said, "You're lucky you feel you have roots someplace. I've been yanked out of so many places. Just when I get to feeling I might belong somewhere, my dad's renting the U-Haul again."

"Maybe you'll stay here," Laura said with an unspoken undertone that said she hoped Megan would.

"Well, like I said, that sort of depends on my dad."

"Perhaps," Laura said cryptically. "Perhaps."

From there, she started into what felt like a long list of questions she had about Megan. What about the kids there? Whom had Megan hung out with—other musicians? Did she have a lot of relatives, besides Mom and Dad and Abe? What about cousins and uncles and aunts? Grandparents?

Megan wasn't used to people being so interested in her and it was flattering. Plus, something about the casual way Laura asked questions put her at ease. She never once felt as though she was being interrogated, or even interviewed—just that Laura found her extremely interesting. The time flew by, and then, suddenly, she realized they were driving up her street.

"It's right over there," Megan said, pointing at the house.

"I know," Laura said, pulling into the driveway.

But how *did* she know? Megan wondered.

"We'll see each other soon," Laura said as Megan hopped out of the car.

"For sure," Megan said. "Maybe we could make plans to get together."

"Oh, I'm not much good at plans," Laura said, pushing her black Wayfarer sunglasses up her nose. "Let's just say I'll find you." She put the car in gear, then looked back up at Megan. "Nice meeting you. I've got a feeling we're going to be real friends. Friends for a long, long time. You know what I mean?"

Megan nodded, feeling happier than she had in a long time. Secure. Taken care of.

Her mom was making peanut butter and chocolate chip cookies when Megan came through the kitchen door. This was her Saturday afternoon "World's Greatest Mother" project. "The one thing that makes me feel like June Cleaver," as her mom put it.

"Did you get your makeup?" she asked Megan, a little distractedly. She was wrapped up in getting her cookie ingredient measurements right, and keeping Abe from beating the cabinets with a wooden spoon he was carrying around, energetically whacking at things.

"Oh," Megan said, realizing she'd left the bag from the drugstore on the floor of Laura's car. "No, I didn't really find what I was looking for." She wasn't sure why, but she didn't want to have to deal with any questions about Laura. Not now. Not just yet.

Up in her room, she put on her Walkman and zoned out. She needed to think. She gradually realized that

31

the conversation she'd thought had been the beginning of some big friendship had been entirely one-sided. Laura had found out about a hundred things about Megan while Megan still knew zero, nada, zip about Laura or The Band. She still had no answers to the million questions she'd been accumulating. Like where did these Band members come from? Where did they live? Where were their houses and parents and brothers and sisters?

She leapt out of bed and went into her parents' bedroom, grabbing the phone book from their nightstand. She couldn't find any Santino, as in Joey. Or any Frederick, as in James. No Eng either. There was a Sam Hunter, but she knew he was a retired guy with no kids because he came to do their yardwork and lived by himself a block over. She finally found a Conroy, but when she called and asked for Shane, a woman told her, "You must have the wrong number. Nobody here by that name."

The next morning on their way to school together, Megan tried Iris again.

"They don't live in town, do they?" she said. There was no point saying she meant The Band. Iris knew what she meant.

"I'd think you'd know all about them by now," Iris said. "Riding around with Laura Hunter in her 'Vette and all. I saw you guys whizzing by. Surely she must've told you all The Band's deep, dark secrets."

"She didn't tell me anything. She *asked* questions— about a million and one—and I, like a total dolt, answered every one of them. And still know nothing about them."

"Exactly how they want it, I'm sure," Iris said.

"Come on, then," Megan pleaded. "At least tell me what you know."

Iris sighed a huge sigh of exasperation, like an actress in a bad play.

"Okay. Somebody told me once that they're from Arlene. It's this little town way out in the desert somewhere. Out past the Blue Mesa. But nobody knows for sure. They just seem to be around town in the late afternoon, into the night. Then, by morning, they've disappeared into thin air."

Megan felt something cold slide through her, like a thin drip of mercury.

"Yeah," Iris was going on. "Why don't you ask your new, good friend Laura to meet you for breakfast some morning? I'd like to see that."

"What do you mean?" Megan said, turning to Iris to see if she'd been joking.

"Just a little theory I have," Iris said. "Nothing I can prove. Yet."

4

"Oh, *Mom*," Megan said, exhaling into a sigh. "Can I just try this on?" She had come across the World's Most Terrific Shirt. Of course, she'd have to admit that almost every time she went shopping, she found the World's Most Terrific something.

Her mother had the night off and they were out at the mall together—"malling." It was one of their favorite things to do. Most of the time they didn't even buy anything, just looked around and window-shopped and got ice cream at the 31 Flavors. When she was younger—like two or three years ago—Megan wouldn't have been caught dead shopping with her mother. Now, though, these expeditions seemed like chances for them to spend time together.

This recent closeness, Megan supposed, was partly about her growing up. But she wasn't the only one changing. Her mother was different ever since they'd moved to Blue Mesa—in a better mood. Actually, the family had moved here partly because of Megan's mother. She'd grown up in this part of Southern California. When she had started getting depressed by all the moving around they were doing, her doctor suggested the family move back closer to her home.

And it seemed to have worked. Now they were living less than fifty miles from the ranch where she was brought up. Even the weather, which felt like the inside of a dry oven to Megan, just made her mom smile in a blissed-out way filled with nostalgia.

"In the summer, you could always fry an egg on these old streets," she'd say. Megan could never figure why anyone would *want* to fry an egg on a street, but she didn't say anything.

But, although her mother was happier, she was not so happy that she could ignore their hard financial realities. Which, Megan knew, didn't include her buying this shirt.

Her mother plucked at its price tag, and within a nanosecond shook her head. "Get real," she said to Megan. "We'd need to take out a loan to afford this shirt. Besides, it's black. Why not look at some pastels, or bright colors. Black is so . . . so . . ."

"So incredibly cool," came a low, throaty voice behind them. They both turned.

It was Laura, and with her, Shane. As usual, they were looking ultrahip, and of course, both were wearing black. On them, the color was a dazzling contrast to their blond hair—his a sort of dirty blond, hers almost white—and their eerie, arctic blue eyes. With a rush of embarrassment, Megan wondered if her mother could see the connection between the way Shane and Laura looked, and her wanting this black shirt. She wondered if her mom could see she was shamelessly copying their look. To cover, she rushed into a fumbling round of introductions, which were even more awkward because of her hardly knowing either of them, particularly Shane, whom she'd barely been introduced to herself.

But Laura was acting as if they were already great friends. "You would look *excellent* in this shirt," she said warmly, lifting the material with the tips of her fingers. "Wouldn't she?" She turned to Shane, who seemed to be hanging back a little, which seemed odd. He was supposed to be the leader of The Band, its dominant energy force, according to Iris. At the moment, though, he looked almost as though he was hiding like a little kid, standing just behind Laura, turning his face away from the rest of them.

"Are you two juniors, like Megan?" her mother asked them as she replaced the shirt with the others on the rack. "I haven't met any of her friends from Mojave yet, except Iris."

"Oh, we don't go to Mojave," Laura said quickly, lightly, offering no further information, then sliding smoothly off the subject. "You're not going to buy that shirt?!"

"It's a little out of our price range, I'm afraid," Megan's mother said.

"Mine, too, actually," Laura said and laughed. "I was just hoping that if I couldn't have it, one of my friends could." Megan felt a little warm flush go through her as Laura claimed her as a friend. She'd expected to go through the standard months of loneliness before she hooked up with any new friends here, but it looked as if that wasn't going to happen this time. She wondered if her mother was noticing how popular she was already, but she seemed fixated on Shane. She was practically staring at him, while he seemed to be ducking her gaze at every turn. What was going on with the two of them?

"Go up to the third level, to that shop, The Attic," Laura suggested helpfully. "It's a great store," she continued in a sugar-sweet voice. "They'll have something cool, but cheaper. Come on. We're not doing anything special. Shane and I can show you where it is." Megan noticed Shane giving Laura a subtle shake of the head, clearly meaning no.

Laura nodded back, just as subtly, to show she'd gotten his message, then looked at her watch. "Oh, darn, we can't. I forgot I have a dentist appointment. We'll have to leave you two to your shopping, I'm afraid," Laura said, pointing Megan and her mother toward The Attic.

"Ahhh," Shane turned and said very casually as they were walking off, "we're sort of having a little party. Saturday night."

"Yeah," Laura finished for him. "We'd like it if you came."

"Oh . . . well," Megan said, caught off guard by the invitation. "Well . . . sure. Where?"

"Oh, well, it's kind of a hard-to-find place," Laura said.

"We'll come by for you," Shane said.

"Around eight?" Laura said, not bothering to wait for an answer, just assuming the answer would be yes.

"Hmmm," her mother said as they watched Laura and Shane walk away.

"Hmmm what?" Megan said. She didn't know what she hoped her mother would say. In a way, she felt almost seduced by Laura and Shane and the whole idea of The Band, and incredibly flattered by their attention to her. In another way, though, she was terrified of everything she didn't know about them, and was almost hoping her mother would say she couldn't go to the party.

"Well, I'm not sure," her mom replied. "There's something odd about them. They don't seem like teenagers. They seem older somehow. It's something about their eyes, as though they've seen a lot. And the boy—Shane—there's something else . . ." She let the sentence trail off into the air.

"What?" Megan said, trying to prod, but her mother just shook her head.

"I don't know. There's something oddly familiar about him. As though I've met him before somewhere. Oh, forget it. I'm probably imagining things."

Late that night, after Megan had finished her homework and was lying in the dark with her headphones on, listening to her new Whitney Houston tape, she saw the light from the hallway flood in as her mother opened the door. She came and sat down on the edge of the bed. Megan slipped her headphones off and the music faded to a tiny, buzzing version of itself.

"What's up?" she asked her mom. It had been quite a few years since she had come to tuck Megan in.

"The boy," her mother said haltingly, nervously. "The boy at the mall today."

"Shane. What about him?"

"Remember I told you he looked familiar, but I couldn't place him? Then tonight it came to me. He looks just like this guy I had a blind date with when I was a sophomore in high school. Just before we moved away from here. My cousin Francie fixed me up with him. He lived near her, miles away from us. I can't even remember the name of the town anymore. But I've always remembered his name. Shane. Because it was so unusual, and because he was so good-looking, I guess. That long blond hair. Those ice blue eyes. The same as your friend. Peculiar, eh?"

At first, Megan didn't know what to say. When she exhaled, she realized she'd been holding her breath for some time. Then it came to her.

"It was probably his dad! Shane's probably named after his father! Probably looks just like him, too. You know. Spitting image. Chip off the old block."

Her mother nodded, and then actually did tuck Megan in a little.

"Of course. You're right," she said as she stood up. "That's got to be it. Well, next time you see him, ask him if he's Shane Junior, and if so, tell him to pass on a hello to his dad for me." She sounded so casual, and was letting the whole thing go so easily. Still, somehow Megan could tell her mother didn't believe a word of what she was saying.

When her mother left the room, shutting the door behind her, Megan was dropped back into total darkness, but not the usual cozy darkness of her bedroom. She closed her eyes, then opened them, but the darkness was the same. It had a cool, damp, eerie cast to it. She was all by herself in this dark place, somewhere her parents and friends like Iris couldn't follow. But there *was* someone waiting there for her, beckoning. She could hear Laura's voice calling softly to her, then Shane's, then the others in The Band. "Megan," they sighed in unison. And then she felt their hands on her, pulling her softly, further into the dead, airless dark. She tried to shake them off, but she had no strength to fight with. In desperation she screamed "Nooooo!"

Suddenly her room was flooded with light.

"What is it, honey?" She recognized her father's voice and sat up in bed. "I was just walking past and heard you scream. You must have been having a nightmare."

"Oh," Megan said in a low voice, almost a whisper. "Right." But she knew it hadn't been any nightmare. You have to be asleep to have nightmares. And she'd been awake—dead awake.

By seven on Saturday night, Megan had been rifling through her closet for half an hour with U2 singing to her from the speakers of her CD player. She pulled clothes from the closet and her dresser drawers, trying them on, then tossing them on the bed until she finally settled on what she was wearing now—black jeans, purple high-tops and a purple T-shirt. She could have worn a black T-shirt, but worried that would make her look a little too eager. She wanted to seem cool and independent, her own person, but still the kind of person The Band would want to hang out with. *If* she decided she wanted to hang out with them. She couldn't remember ever being so ambivalent about anything.

She slouched in front of the mirror on her closet door. *Perfect,* she thought—a thought followed almost immediately by Abe's tiny, gravelly voice saying, "Batman."

She turned toward the doorway where he was being held in the arms of her mother, who added her own comment on Megan's appearance.

"You do look a little overnocturnal."

"Hunh?" Megan said.

"You know. A creature of the night. What color lipstick is that? It looks so pale and ghoulish."

"Oh, it's just peach with tan over it," Megan said. Jenny Gonzales had come up to her at her locker a few days earlier and handed her the bag of makeup she'd left in Laura's car.

"Nice shade of lipstick," she'd said as she was walking away. "Laura and I tried it on. Hope you don't mind."

Megan had stood there a moment after Jenny was gone, trying to decide whether she minded or not.

Megan's mother, although basically cool, had this cheery idea of how Megan ought to dress. Bright colors and pastels. Like the sassy, smart-aleck daughter on some TV sitcom. Which just wasn't Megan. She was grateful when her mother moved onto another subject.

"When are your friends coming by for you?"

"Eight."

"And you'll be home by midnight?"

"*Mom*."

"You heard me. I don't know enough about these kids. At first I was thinking of simply not letting you go tonight, but I know how hard it is for you when we move to a new town. Making friends and all. So I don't want to stand in your way. On the other hand, they could be werewolves and whisk you off to Transylvania."

"So how's a curfew going to help?"

"Oh, the werewolf vans never leave before twelve-thirty. It's a well-known fact. So if you're home by midnight, I don't have to worry."

Underneath her mom's kidding around, Megan could hear that she was worried, but trying to keep calm. Which meant Megan had better not push it about the curfew. No matter how uncool it was, she was going to have to get someone at the party to bring her home early.

"I come, too," Abe said. He was now crawling around on the bedroom floor, looking for stuff of Megan's he could get into.

"Yeah, right," Megan said. "Please say yes, Mom. Let me bring Abe to the party with me." Her mother laughed, and the tension was broken. Now she could go off to the party and not have to spend the night worrying that her mother was home worrying about her.

It was twenty past eight by the time the doorbell rang. Megan was beginning to think she'd been forgotten, left behind. But when she opened the door, there was Shane Conroy leaning against the porch pillar, his blond hair loose tonight, a burnt-down cigarette between his thumb and forefinger.

"Hey," he said from behind sunglasses, even though it was deep into dusk by the time he and Laura arrived to pick Megan up. "You're looking good."

"My party mode," Megan said, flicking one of her dangly sun-moon-star earrings with a finger. She shouted a quick "bye" back into the house as she shut the front door behind her and headed toward the black Camaro, which was was idling in her driveway.

She wondered if the whole Band was inside, like those cars at the circus that hold a hundred clowns. But there was only Laura, who didn't even say hi, just smiled at Megan as though they were so close they were beyond obvious gestures, like spoken hellos. Megan sort of liked this, and at the same time was sort of spooked by it.

"Cool car," Megan said, trying to start up some sort of conversation. "You guys all have such great old cars. Where do you get them?"

"Well, you know," Shane said, "sometimes people misplace these old cars and they just sort of turn up with us, if you get my drift."

"Oh," Megan said.

With the air conditioning roaring and the tinted windows up, Megan felt totally enclosed, enveloped by the car. As they drove along, a tape of songs by a female singer Megan didn't recognize playing out of the car's huge, hidden speakers, she felt more like she was shooting through outer space than just along a highway.

"What's this?" she asked Shane and Laura, meaning the music.

"Surely you jest," Laura said. "Carole King."

" *'Tapestry,'* " Shane added. "Awesome record. Best album of the year."

"What year?" Megan teased, but clearly Shane felt caught.

"Oh, well, whatever year it came out," he said, but his voice was full of bluff.

"1972," Laura said, flatly, as if picking a card off the deck and snapping it faceup on the table.

Shane drove, Laura sat next to him, and they passed a cigarette back and forth between them, silently. Once she leaned over and blew smoke in his ear. Hardly any of the kids Megan had known in Boulder had smoked, and not very many at Mojave seemed to either. In Megan's mind, smoking was something from the past, something people did in old movies. But from what she'd seen, most of The Band members smoked. And it seemed as though they did it because they thought it looked cool, the way people used to before everyone got hip to cigarettes and started hating them like poison.

She pressed her nose against the window next to her and tried to see out, but couldn't spot any recognizable landmarks. "Uh, where *is* the party anyway?"

"Out at the Blue Mesa," Shane said, turning briefly to look back at her.

"I told you we like to hang there," Laura said. "It's far enough out that no one hassles us."

"In case things get too wild and loud?" Megan guessed.

"Or too quiet," Shane said cryptically.

What did that mean? Megan wondered as she watched him look over at Laura and smile slightly, as though they were partners in something so deep and secret that most of it went unspoken.

"Will Toby be there? I haven't seen him all week. I heard he had a cold."

"Yeah," Shane said. "He's been Nyquilling, but we persuaded him it would be a good thing if he got out of bed and drove out tonight. We have plans to discuss with him."

He didn't elaborate on what these plans might be, and Megan was getting to know The Band well enough not to bother to ask what anything they said or did meant. She could drive herself crazy wondering, but they were clearly not—not *yet* anyway—going to let her in on their secrets.

The party was already in gear when they arrived. A semicircle of black cars were parked at the foot of the mesa, their parking lights creating a bluish yellow haze in the middle of the pitch darkness.

Shane had the driver's-side window rolled down, and when they pulled to a stop, Joey Santino reached in to high-five him. Jenny Gonzales was hanging all over Joey. Megan guessed they must be a couple.

"What's happening?" Shane asked in a numb, going-through-the-motions sort of way. There were undercurrents of sadness about Shane that fascinated Megan. Her feelings about him were confusing. She was attracted to him, but he seemed too distant to imagine ever getting close to. Still, she had this intense curiosity about him. She felt as though she was a detective and he was her suspect—only she hadn't figured out yet what his crime was.

"Everybody's getting pretty mellow," Joey said, suddenly not attached to Jenny Gonzales, whom Megan saw go over to James and try to pull him up to dance . The romantic arrangements of The Band seemed to be very fluid.

Megan could hear the raspy voice of Rod Stewart singing "Maggie May" coming out of a huge boom box propped on a boulder. She liked Rod Stewart. Her parents had a couple of his albums. But didn't The Band ever listen to any *new* music?

Lots of kids were dancing, which was real unusual. Maybe kids here were different, but dancing—especially the sort of disco dancing almost everyone here was doing—was something that had been decidedly uncool back in Colorado.

She recognized a lot of the kids. Jenny Gonzales, of course. Ron Mason from her cooking class. Antonia Greco from phys ed. Zoe Freed had the locker two down from hers, and Ethan Hayes played trumpet in the school orchestra. Each of them was being tended to—at least that's what it looked like—by someone from The Band. It was like fraternity or sorority rush parties she'd seen in movies where the members are busy looking over the crop of candidates, hustling the ones they wanted to sign up.

A distinct nonparticipant in all this was James, who was instead lying on the ground in front of the boulder stretched out on his back, staring up into the night sky, a jug of wine stuck in the sand next to him.

"James is especially mellow," Joey told Megan as he turned up suddenly at her side. She had the feeling she was being passed around, that one Band member or another would be hanging around her at any given moment tonight.

She looked for Toby, and finally spotted him sitting cross-legged up on a low rock formation, deep in conversation with Natalie Eng. He looked up vaguely when Megan caught his eye, and raised a hand in a listless wave. She was crushed.

"Hey," Shane said, suddenly beside her, like a host. "We've got to get you something to drink."

"Do you have any soda?" she asked.

"Uh, I don't think so," he said.

We generally like our liquid refreshment with a little more kick than just carbonation," Laura explained, also now back at Megan's side, as though she was a shepherdess and Megan her sheep. "Like wine."

"Red wine," Shane specified.

Megan basically didn't drink. She'd tried it a couple of times at parties in Colorado. Once she had just gotten incredibly sleepy, and when she woke up, the party was over and someone was shaking her shoulder, asking if she needed a ride home. The other time she had been drinking something called "mimosas," which were delicious going down—like fruit juice and fire and ice. But after the third one, they started coming back up. This happened quite suddenly and all over Cynthia Freely's family room sofa.

After that, she decided drinking probably wasn't for her. She tried to explain this to them.

"That could be a problem," Shane said.

"Throwing up?" Megan said.

"Not joining wholeheartedly in our trivial pursuits," Laura said. "If you're too straight around us, you won't be on our wavelength."

"You'll be in daylight while we're in the night," Shane said, then passed Megan the open bottle they'd all been sharing.

Megan put it to her lips and drank the smallest sip she could. The taste was sharp and sour at the same time. She winced. "Not my cup of tea, really," she said. She tried to keep it light but at the same time be clear that she didn't want to be forced into being someone she wasn't.

"You'll get used to it," Laura said. "It grows on you."

For some reason, this sounded like a threat. There was something edgy underlying all the supposed "mellowness" at this party, but Megan couldn't exactly put her finger on it.

She looked up and noticed Laura looking at her in the strangest way.

"Isn't it incredible how much she looks like Marnie?" Laura asked Shane.

He nodded, didn't say anything for the longest time, then came as close as Megan had yet seen to smiling, and said, "Yeah, it makes me happy."

"Uh," Megan interrupted, "Marnie who?"

"Oh," Shane said. "She was a friend of ours who . . ."

"Who we've lost touch with," Laura quickly finished the sentence for him.

Finally, Toby, who'd been talking with Natalie so long that Megan had begun to think they were a couple, came down off his rock and joined them. Someone had made a fire out of brushwood. Now that the sun was completely down, the desert was beginning to cool off fast. Megan sat down close to the fire and, when Toby came up beside her and joined her, she waited a while before she said, "I hear you've been on the bench with a cold all week." She didn't really want to talk to him if he wasn't all that interested in talking to her.

"Yeah," he said listlessly. "I've still got it a little." He sniffled as if to back up his statement. "The orchestra surviving without me?"

"Barely," she said. "We limp along, but our hearts aren't in it without the presence of your talents."

She knew it wasn't the wittiest remark ever uttered in the civilized world, but she *was* a little surprised that he didn't even smile.

Instead, he just nodded and said, "I'll be back on Monday."

She was beginning to wonder why she'd been excited that he was going to be here tonight. The way he was acting, you'd think their connection was that he'd once delivered a pizza to her house. Or they'd been to the same orthodontist and seen each other in the waiting room a couple of times. He didn't seem anything like the person she'd gone out with the weekend before. Girls sometimes talked about guys doing this—acting one way one time, then turning off totally by the next time you see them. But this had never happened to her, and so Megan was really hurt by it.

49

"Isn't Leslie Tellman in the orchestra, too?" Natalie asked, lighting her cigarette off the old-fashioned Zippo lighter Shane was holding out toward her, cupping his hand around the flame. Natalie was wearing a very hot outfit—black spandex skirt, tube top, and a black leather "girl gang" jacket. Every time Megan blinked, it seemed The Band had broken down and regrouped into a new set of couples. It was kind of like a sexual kaleidoscope.

"Yeah," Toby said. "She plays French horn." He had the same zomboid tone he'd had talking to her. She began to think his peculiar mood didn't have anything to do with her, that something was just really "off" about him in general tonight.

"*She* might be a candidate." Natalie was talking about Leslie Tellman.

"I don't think so," Laura said, shaking her head, exhaling a rush of smoke through her nose. "She's got a boyfriend she's marrying as soon as they're out of high school, plus she works nights at the Jumbo Donut. She's on the soccer team. Basically, the girl is booked."

"We need friends whose schedules are more flexible," Shane said to Megan, as if he were really explaining something to her, as if he were making sense.

"Well, that's not Leslie," Laura said. "Leslie is filofaxed to the max. She's scheduled from here until about when she turns thirty."

"Turning to the underscheduled," James said, focusing like a zoom lens, in and out until he had things unblurred, "Simon Whitley. He's all over me like a cold sweat lately." Simon Whitley was a huge boy who was a chemistry whiz. Everyone said he performed secret experiments in a laboratory in his basement, but Megan figured it was just the sort of thing regular kids say about weird-looking kids.

Guys like James—with their sarcastic, supercritical attitude toward everyone else—scared Megan, made her wonder what they were saying about her the moment her back was turned.

"Simon Whitley," Natalie said, curling one side of her upper lip. "*Please.* We may need numbers, but we have our standards."

"I just said he wanted in," James said. "I didn't say he had a chance of *getting* in."

Getting in what? Megan wondered, but not really. Without having things spelled out for her, she pretty much knew. What she didn't know now, though, was what getting into The Band meant.

A lizard skittered out of the darkness surrounding them into their perimeter of light. In an instant, James came out of his fog and moved like lightning, flipping over onto his stomach directly in front of the lizard, locking gazes with it. The lizard froze in its tracks, seemingly paralyzed by James's stare. Everyone just watched as if it was a mildly amusing parlor trick. To Megan, though, if felt creepier than that, and scarier, as though James—and the others as well—were like lounging lions, with power they were holding in reserve for something. But what?

"Anyone want some nice lizard sushi?" James said, still holding the creature prisoner to his stare, pulling a jackknife from the back pocket of his jeans.

"Let him go," Shane said quietly, but with utter authority. It was clear that, as far as The Band was concerned, his word went.

Megan had a few more sips of wine, taking a small one whenever the bottle came around. She didn't want to seem snobbish. They might not invite her to another one of their parties. She was so unused to drinking that her head began to hum a little and the scene of the party took on a dreamy haze. At one point she was pretty sure she heard Shane ask, "Are we set for Toby's initiation?"

"We need to wait a bit," Natalie said. "Until the moon turns full, a week from Friday night."

"At the cave," James said, draping a long arm across Toby's shoulders. "Scared?"

Toby shook his head, but Megan noticed he didn't say anything.

"Everything's a passage, Toby," Shane said. "Nothing stays the same even if you want it to. Might as well go with the change."

James lit two cigarettes. Megan watched him, wondering what he was doing until he pulled one from between his lips and handed it to her.

She shook her head. "I'd just cough all over the place and embarrass myself."

"No bad habits," he mused, dropping the cigarette onto the sand, crushing it with the heel of his boot. "We're going to have to do something about that."

Megan felt alternately as though she was being courted by The Band and held at arm's length from them. It was as if they wanted to know everything about her—to capture her like a little prize—but didn't want her to know about them, about who they really were and what they were really up to.

What was their big secret? It was becoming clear that there was one. And if they wanted to keep it, needed to be so mysterious, then why didn't they just keep to themselves, why did they want to drag other kids like her and Toby and Jennifer in?

Suddenly, her thoughts were interrupted by what looked like a scuffle over in the shadow of the mesa. It looked like the kind of tense encounters guys sometimes had around the sidelines of football games or burger joint parking lots. Menace and muted terror. Somebody being ganged up on.

Through her haze, she saw it was Ethan Hayes, caught in a tight circle made up of Shane and James and Joey. Whatever they were saying to him, it was clear he was freaked out by it. Suddenly, he broke free and ran out of the lit circle of the party, through the periphery where the cars were parked, into the thick darkness of the desert night.

No one ran after him. Everyone just stood there, frozen. Watching and listening, but for what?

"Shouldn't we go and try to find him?" Megan finally asked.

"He made the decision to leave," Shane said, ice in his voice. "So he takes his chances in the desert."

"He'll probably find the highway and hitch a ride into town," Laura said in a tone clearly meant to smooth things over and put the party back on track.

"Yeah," James said sarcastically, "He'll probably get back. No problem."

Luckily, it was getting close to her curfew. Laura reluctantly drove Megan home when no one else could believe she really had to be back by midnight. "We wouldn't want your parents mad at us," Laura had said and took Shane's keys and Megan's hand, as though she were a total baby.

Megan blamed it on her mom, but was secretly glad to be going home. Whatever had gone on with Ethan was a total creep-out. What could have driven him into the unseen terrors of desert darkness rather than stay at the party?

"Don't be frightened by what happened back there," Laura said, as if reading Megan's mind.

Megan didn't say anything, just let the hum of the air conditioning fill the space inside the car.

"Sometimes we make an offer to someone we like, and they're not interested in what we're offering. Ethan wasn't interested. That's all."

It was as though Laura was trying to make it seem Ethan had turned down a candy bar or stick of gum. But running into the wilderness wasn't how anyone said no thanks.

When Laura pulled up in front of Megan's house, Megan still couldn't find words, couldn't sort out her feelings about the night, and Ethan, and the lizard, and Toby, and The Band.

"Why don't you just give me your number and I'll give you a call in a few days," she said to Laura, pulling her little address book out of her backpack. She held her pen poised over a fresh, blank line in the *H* section for Hunter.

"Oh," Laura said. "You won't need any phone numbers for us." She reached across Megan and opened the door for her. "We'll always be in touch. We'll always find you."

6

By Monday, everything seemed to have returned to normal—or almost normal. Toby was back in school and at orchestra practice he was his old self. When Megan tried to press about the odd, distant way he'd acted toward her at the party, he just ducked.

"I really shouldn't even have been there," he said. "I was still down with that lousy cold. Sorry if I seemed a little strange."

"You didn't seem strange," she told him. "You seemed like a stranger."

"Well then, I'll just have to make that up to you somehow," he said, smiling shyly and taking her hand, holding it for a little while beneath her music stand, so Mr. Sneed wouldn't see. Toby was just the way she remembered him from the great Saturday night they'd spent together. She was mystified.

Ethan Hayes was at orchestra practice, too. Looking gray, like someone who'd come back from being sick for a while. After Toby had left, Megan went over to talk with him.

"Hey," she said. "You okay?"

"Yeah, fine."

"I was just curious."

"Well, now you've satisfied your curiosity."

It was clear he didn't want to talk about what had happened at the party, but Megan couldn't let it go.

"You got back okay, I gather," she said, stating the obvious.

"Yeah, but it took me half the night. When you're hitchhiking at two in the morning, people tend to think you're a serial killer, or at least someone just escaped from prison. When I finally got picked up, it was by this carload of born-again Christians on their way back from a revival meeting. They spent the whole way back trying to convert me."

"What a night," Megan sympathized.

Ethan's expression turned serious again, and when he spoke, it was in a lowered voice. "Look, I don't know how deep you're in with them, but bad things are going to happen. If I were you, I'd get out now." He didn't have to specify the "them"; they both knew whom he was talking about.

She nodded.

"Can you tell me more?"

She saw his face shut down.

"I really don't want to talk about it. They've got their secrets, and they don't like people spilling them. I just want to be out of it all. You should want the same thing. That's all I can say."

Megan watched him leave the music room and touched her face. It was hot. She knew she should take to heart what he was telling her, or not quite telling her. But there was still so much about The Band that was magnetic. And they were so great to her, the group of friends she'd always wanted, but never stayed in any one place long enough to find. Now that she had found this, she hated to give it all up just because a couple of people—Iris and now

Ethan—didn't like them and told her she shouldn't either.

She shook her hair back over her shoulders as she walked out into the hall, as though the gesture would shake her free of the clammy feeling the conversation with Ethan had left her with.

When she got out in front of school, Natalie and Laura were waiting for her in Laura's Corvette. It was odd that even though the car was a convertible and most days around Blue Mesa were certainly hot enough to have the top down, Laura never seemed to. Today she and Natalie were lounging deep inside the depths of the sports car, behind the tinted panes of its windows, chilled out in its hyper air conditioning, smoking the unfiltered cigarettes the Band members favored.

When Megan got close to the car, they both opened their eyes, as if they'd felt her approach on some inner radar. Laura hopped out of the car.

"Come on," she said to Megan, laughing, "you drive."

"B-b-but . . ." Megan started to come up with all the reasons she really shouldn't be driving someone else's Corvette, but Laura pulled her by the hand while Natalie—who was just small enough to make this possible—hopped into the boot behind the seats. "Where are we going?" Megan asked.

"The mall, my dear," Natalie said from the back, over the roar of the 'Vette's engine.

"To get you some proper clothes," Laura said. "A touch of black, perhaps."

At the mall, Megan tried to stop the two of them from filling her arms with a sea of black—jeans and baggy cotton pants and T-shirts—even the washed silk shirt she had been looking at with her mother.

"You guys!" she said, laughing, "this is all great and I appreciate your fashion guidance, but I can't afford this stuff!"

"Oh, don't worry about that," Laura said. "Just let us know what you like and we'll take care of getting it for you."

"But I don't really need a black wardrobe, cool as it is."

"Oh, but you *do*," Laura said. "For starters, Toby's initiation is coming up in a couple of weeks. You have to dress right for important occasions. And if you're going to be hanging out with us, there are going to be quite a few 'basic black' occasions."

Megan saw this as an opportunity.

"Now that you mention it," she said, trying to sound casual as she headed toward the fitting rooms, "just what exactly *is* this initiation anyway?"

"Toby's decided to come over to us," Natalie said cryptically.

"But what does that mean?" Megan asked.

She watched Natalie and Laura exchange looks that were so heavy with meaning they weighed about a ton. Finally Natalie said, "You may have noticed, Megan, that we're a little different from the other kids around here."

The understatement of the year! Megan thought.

"We stay to ourselves and do things our own way, but occasionally we see someone of promise and potential—someone like you—and we want to bring them into our circle. Toby's another person we consider extremely worthwhile. We want him to join us, to really be one of us. But in order to do that, he has to come over from the other side."

"What other side?"

"Oh," Laura said, running a hand through her tumble of pale blonde hair, "how can I put it? It's as though we belong to the night and the rest of the world exists in the daylight. To really join us means moving on from the daylight life and the friends you have there."

"I just got to Blue Mesa," Megan said. "I hardly *have* any friends except you guys."

"Then coming over should be easier for you," Natalie said.

"When the time comes," Laura added. "You don't have to think about that quite yet. We'll know when you're ready and then we'll let *you* know. Now," she said, standing up, holding a skimpy black dress up by its hanger. "Let's see how you look in this little number."

"All right. Come on in with me," Megan said, nodding toward the open door to the fitting room.

"No, that's okay," Laura said. "We'll just wait out here."

"It's okay. I've been in sports all my life. I gave up being modest years ago," Megan assured them.

"Really, we'd rather stay out here and have you model for us," Laura said.

"Yeah," Natalie added, "mirrors kind of give us the creeps."

Megan tried to figure out what this meant. Why would mirrors give anyone as cool-looking as Laura and Natalie the creeps? Then she decided to just forget all this sort of stuff for the rest of the day—all The Band's oddities and peculiarities and all the dire warnings against them—and just enjoy this little treat her new friends were giving her. She went in and tried on everything they'd picked, and when the three of them had settled on a pair of jeans, a T-shirt and the silk one, too, Megan was told to go on ahead out into the mall.

"We'll take care of things from here," Laura said, giving her a gentle push toward the door of the store. Maybe this meant they didn't want her to stand there while they bought her clothes, but Megan suspected that, more likely, they were going to boost the items Megan had selected. Megan had never shoplifted anything in her life and the whole idea made her nervous. She couldn't stop them because she wasn't sure that's what they were doing. One thing for sure—she didn't want to be around in case they *were* stealing her "presents." She took their orders gladly, zipping out into the mall as fast as she could without breaking into a run.

While she was waiting on a bench next to a fountain, she was surprised to see Iris coming toward her, walking along in her brisk, agitated way. She didn't know which she wanted less—for Iris to see she was with Natalie and Laura, or for them to see her chatting with Iris, who was not exactly the coolest person in Blue Mesa, not exactly the person you'd want The Band to think was your best buddy.

Then she was embarrassed at herself for being so superficial. Iris was a neat person even if she did look a little peculiar. Well, maybe slightly more than a *little* peculiar today, since she was wearing glasses with tiger stripe frames, and had her hair pulled back on the sides in plastic, little kid barrettes that said "Iris."

"I've got to talk with you," Iris said. "I've got something to show you. About your new friends.

Can you meet me at the public library after school tomorrow?"

Megan was getting a little tired of Iris's cloak-and-dagger attitude, and coming off her chat with Ethan, had about her quota for the day of murky, sinister, whispered conversations. Still, something in the urgency of her tone persuaded her that this really was something important, and so she sighed and said, "Okay."

And then looked back up just in time to see Natalie and Laura coming across the mall toward them.

"Oh boy, the Terrifying Twins," Iris said. "I can't believe you're hanging out with them."

For their part, Laura and Natalie were looking at her and Iris as if boring through them with X-ray vision and infrared lenses. It was a little scary. Obviously they were determined to know what was going on.

"Hi guys," Megan said, trying to sound casual. "Have you met my neighbor, Iris Wojack?" They nodded at each other like snakes coiled in separate baskets.

"Iris and I are working on a social studies assignment together," Megan lied. "We need to do some research—on young people from different cultures, how their customs are not like ours—and we've got to get started pronto. Tomorrow. Right?" She nodded toward Iris.

"Yeah, right."

"Well, have fun," Laura said, "but don't believe everything you read in books." It was spooky; it was as though she knew what they were really going to be doing at the library. Which was double weird because Megan didn't know herself yet.

This was Megan's first trip to the Blue Mesa Public Library. It was a cloudless afternoon and the sun came through the venetian-blinded windows in stripes that seemed to hold aloft thousands of dust motes.

Page dust, she thought idly, *from all the pages of all the books resting in here.*

As she came in, she looked around for Iris but didn't see her, so she kept walking through the newest section of the library to the farthest back and oldest part. Here the shelves were of dark wood, groaning under the weight of all the books jammed into them, and the aisles narrowed and the air grew stuffy.

She was walking slowly down one of these aisles, passing through Biography, then Military History, when she heard a raspy whisper, the sort of whisper that's about equal to a shout.

"Hey!"

She turned to see Iris pressing a finger to her lips.

"Oh Iris. Come on. You've been reading too many Nancy Drews. What is this—*The Signpost of the Sinister Secret?*"

62

"You're not going to be joking anymore when you see what I've found."

"Yeah, right," Megan said, rolling her eyes for good measure.

"Something *they're* not going to be happy I'm showing you." Having said this, Iris looked furtively up and down the aisle.

"Iris, maybe I should get you a trench coat and some dark glasses. So you won't be recognized in the . . . in the *public library*!" She grabbed Iris with tickling fingers, but none of her teasing worked.

"Quit fooling around. We've got serious business to attend to," Iris said. "Come here."

Megan followed her into a small room at the very back of the library. There, lying open on an old wooden table, was a large book, its pages yellowed, its binding sprung. Megan picked it up by the front cover to see its title.

"*The World of the Occult?*"

"Here," Iris motioned for Megan to pull up a chair while she did the same. "You see, here it is. They're revenants."

"*Who?*"

"The Band, of course."

"What on earth are revens . . . ?"

"Revenants. And 'on earth' might not be the correct context. Revenants are sort of second cousins to vampires. They're all in the great family of the Undead."

"Come again?"

"Undead, Megan," Iris said matter-of-factly, as though she had just said The Band members were all right-handed, or liked cheeseburgers.

Megan's first impulse was to crack another joke, to tease Iris for coming up with something so absurd, something out of a supermarket newspaper. But something stopped her. Instead, she watched her friend's finger run under the print in the book, as she read aloud, softly.

"The Undead have died, but they've returned because they've not been allowed to go to their final rest. Their deaths were untimely. They died before the time they were supposed to go. And so they inhabit a wandering state, unable to rest here or in the beyond. They are doomed to roam the earth, which is why they are characteristically restless. They abhor the day and appear mostly at night. In broad daylight, they shield their eyes from sunlight, which is painful to them."

"The shades," Megan breathed.

"They favor the color black—in garments, horses, and carriages."

Megan gave Iris a "get real" look. "Carriages? Garments?"

"Hey," Iris countered, "they didn't have Corvettes back when this book was written."

"Okay. Go ahead."

"They are lonely in their wanderings and so search relentlessly for recruits, innocent victims— usually other lonely souls—to join them."

"How do they do that?" Megan said, half afraid, half insulted at being referred to as a lonely soul.

"I don't know. That's about all this book has on revenants."

Megan felt swamped with thoughts, as if she had walked into quicksand and was being pulled down. She could see so many connections between what Iris had just read to her and The Band. She began to run through these connections in her mind, trying them out.

They were too bizarre to be possible, too creepy to think about. And for sure too crazy to talk with Iris about—at least now. And so—even though she hated herself as she did it, knowing how much work and concern Iris had put in on her behalf—Megan brushed Iris off.

"Get a life. This is Southern California in the '90s. The *nineteen* nineties. Not the 1800s in Transylvania."

Of course, Iris couldn't be right about The Band, Megan thought. It was just that she saw too many horror movies on video with all her geeky brothers. Her imagination was running wild. Plus she was probably jealous of Megan—getting in with such an incredibly cool crowd practically within minutes of arriving on the scene while Iris had been in Blue Mesa all her life and had about two friends total.

For the next week or so, Megan avoided Iris, stopped driving herself crazy wondering about The Band, and just sat back and enjoyed the whole thing. She let Shane pick her up from school and loved it when Laura called her late at night, just before she went to sleep. (That is, just before she, Megan, went to sleep. Megan had the feeling that her bedtime was just the beginning of The Band's evening.) They all seemed to be interested in her, in who she was and what she thought about things, her ideas about life and her future. She had never really had such a devoted bunch of friends before. Why be so suspicious of their motives? Couldn't it be possible they just really liked her?

She would have thought her parents would be happy for her. Before, they were always after her to get out more, meet people, but now that she had friends, they were all of a sudden suspicious.

"Where'd you get those jeans?" her mother asked

when Megan came into the kitchen one morning.

"These? Oh, Natalie and Laura got them for me."

"And the shirt?"

"Yeah."

"And that Swatch?"

"Mom. They're just generous is all." Even as she was saying this, the words sounded hollow in her ears.

"Honey. Friends don't buy each other clothes and watches." These were Megan's exact thoughts, but she couldn't voice them, not now that she'd accepted the presents. She'd avoided wearing the stuff as long as she felt she could; it made her uncomfortable having it. But she didn't want to offend Laura and Natalie.

"Where do they even get the money?"

Megan thought it probably wasn't the best idea to say, "Oh, don't worry, they didn't buy all this stuff for me. They just stole it."

"I don't know," she said instead. "Maybe from their jobs."

"And just what are these high-paying positions that give them enough spare cash to be so generous to their friends?"

Megan didn't have an answer to this.

"Sweetheart, I'm not trying to hassle you, but can't you see there are way too many blanks to be filled in with these kids? You don't even know where they live or what they do all day."

"I know I like them," Megan said, feeling forced onto the defensive. "And they like me. You want me to make friends, and then when I do, they're not good enough for you! Would everybody please just get off my back?"

As she went out the back door, she could hear Abe

stopping in the middle of slurping his oatmeal to say, "I don't see anyone on Megan's back."

Once outside, she felt free, released like a bug from a chloroform jar. Lately with her mom and dad and Abe, she was always dying to escape into what was more and more beginning to seem like her real life—with The Band.

After orchestra practice, Megan and Toby put their instruments in their lockers and headed out of school together. They'd planned to go swimming. Her mom had arranged for Mrs. Hodges to cover for her with Abe.

"So where is this mysterious, secret swimming place?" she asked Toby now.

"Out toward the mountains," he said, tossing her stuff into the backseat of his car, an ancient yellow Toyota he'd resuscitated from a junkyard heap. "It's a little lake in the foothills."

They stopped for Cokes at a gas station and shared a bag of chips as they drove from the desert into the place where the landscape turned greener and less flat. They talked about what a bear Sneed was, making them learn so many hard and completely new numbers for the Christmas concert. Then they talked about movies. They both considered themselves kind of authorities, having watched them ever since they could remember. Megan liked when they agreed on a movie or actor or actress, but she liked even better that when they disagreed, they could have fun arguing from their opposite points of view.

Today the issue was that she adored Meryl Streep while he thought she was mega-affected.

"If they gave Oscars for attitude and posturing, she'd win in a walk," he teased.

67

"At least she gets parts where she can *have* attitude, instead of spending 50 percent of her career trying to get a drooling alien off her spacecraft," Megan said, referring to Toby's status as a diehard Sigourney Weaver fan.

"Touché," he said, reaching over the gear shift to give Megan a pinch in the ribs.

To get back, she tweaked his earlobe.

"Not the one with the earring!" he screeched in mock agony.

The lake was small and bordered by a stand of trees. No one else was there when they arrived. They changed at opposite ends of the "forest," then raced each other into the water, which was deep blue and freezing cold.

"You didn't tell me this part!" Megan screamed when she came up for air.

"I must've forgot," Toby said, diving down, then coming up in front of Megan. "Come here. I'll lend you a little of my body heat."

Like everything else with Toby, kissing him was easy, too. Megan just stood on the soft sand bottom of the lake and enjoyed the blend of sensations—hot and cold mixed, kind of like a hot fudge sundae—the water and Toby's arms around her, their bodies pressing against each other, their cold lips and warm mouths.

"How'd I get so lucky, meeting you right away when I came here?" she said.

"We're cosmic twins," he said. "We knew each other in some past life. We were galley slaves attached to the same oar."

"Water oxen in the same yoke."

"Exactly."

When they felt like they were about to turn blue,

they ran onto the small beach and bundled up in the soft old cotton blankets Toby had brought along.

In spite of her decision not to think about her fears about The Band, Megan felt so close to Toby she wanted to warn him.

"Iris and I found out stuff—about The Band." She told him about the book on the occult at the library, about revenants and the Undead.

"But what does any of that have to to with The Band?"

She sighed with frustration. "I don't know. Maybe she's way off base. I sure hope so. But The Band . . . I mean, look, I'm not saying they're not incredibly cool and all, but you and I both know there is something *distinctly* peculiar about them. I just want to see what we're getting into. I mean, don't you wonder what they mean when they talk about your *initiation*?"

"Shane told me. They're going to do something to me, out at the cave, to make me closer to them, more a part of what they're all about. It's probably just a secret handshake, or something."

"Closer to them? What they're all about? What does any of that mean? You and I don't have to initiate each other to be closer. We just talk and show each other who we are. Like normal people. Why is there all this mystery around them?"

Toby thought for a moment, then said, "Yeah, I understand what you're saying, but the mystery is also part of what makes them so cool. You have to admit they're not like anyone else around here."

"You can say that again."

"And doesn't part of you want to be around them, be part of whatever they've got going, be taken into their aura?"

Megan nodded. She had to agree. "Still, I think we should check them out. I mean they know practically everything about us—Natalie and Laura even want to see my baby album!—and we know *nothing* about them."

"Maybe so," Toby said, unwrapping their blankets and rewrapping them around the two of them so they were in a cocoon together. "But this stuff Iris has come up with sounds way off base. Too farfetched. My guess is there are reasonable explanations for all their little . . . oddities. And we'll find them out as things go along. I'll bet I find out lots more at the initiation."

Megan felt a shudder pass through her and goosebumps formed up and down her arms and legs. She couldn't tell if she was responding to the cold air of the fading afternoon, or to the word *initiation*.

8

Megan told her mother she needed new reeds for her clarinet.

"They don't have anything decent out here in no-man's-land. Mr. Sneed gave us the name of a good music store in Los Angeles."

"I can drive you in on Saturday," her mother offered. "We can take Abe with us."

"Mr. Car Sick? Thanks, but no thanks. I'll just take the bus. It's easy. It leaves from right behind the post office. And he gave us directions. It's just a quick cab ride from the bus station. I won't have to find my way around on public transportation or anything like that." She'd planned this whole pack of lies to allay any worries her mother might come up with. Sometimes she fantasized what her mother would do if she ever told her the whole truth. Like:

"Yeah, Mom. Actually I'm going to L.A. to go to this occult bookshop so I can find out more about The Band, who are probably not just grungy, de-generate, drug-pushing teenagers like you suspect, but are actually Undead."

She'd found out about the bookstore at the public library. She'd gone back by herself, but discovered that the book Iris had dug up was pretty much all they had. She talked with the librarian, an extremely tall, gaunt woman with dark hair piled high on her head, and eyebrows drawn in with a heavy, reddish brown pencil. MRS. DECARLO, her little desk sign said.

"If you need more depth on the subject, I'd recommend this establishment. I know the owner slightly; he's extremely knowledgeable in the area," she'd said, writing on a slip of paper, "Occult Book Shoppe, 17 Luis Street."

"Well, I definitely need more depth in the area," Megan admitted.

"A school paper?" the librarian said, arching one of her penciled-in brows.

"Uh, not exactly," Megan said, and walked out before Mrs. DeCarlo could come up with any more penetrating questions.

After her talk with Toby at the lake, she'd seen a reflection of her own reluctance in his refusal to take a hard look at The Band. Maybe Iris was wrong. Maybe there was nothing to her theory. But if there was, Megan needed to find out, and quick. Before Toby's initiation. She couldn't let her questions slide any longer just because it felt good being courted by The Band. But obviously the library wasn't going to provide the answers she needed.

She slept most of the way to L.A. on the bus. She'd been sleeping either restlessly or not at all for the past few nights, tangled in dreams of vampires and werewolves and zombies in black.

Even with the map she'd brought, it wasn't easy finding Luis Street, which turned out to be a tiny dead-end alley near the beach. Number 17 was a frame-fronted shop wedged between a pizzeria and a laundromat. She pushed open the wooden door and was overcome by the smell of dust and binding glue and the mildew of old pages.

It was hard to tell how big the shop was, so crammed was every available space with books. Books bound in red leather, huge volumes with the covers rotting off. Nothing looked new in here, or even for sale, really. It looked more like someone's private collection.

"May I help you?" came a voice booming out of nowhere. Megan looked around, then up, then finally saw him. He was a huge man, both heavy and tall, looming like a vulture over a railing that ran around a second floor loft full of yet more books.

"Oh, I'm just looking around," she said.

"We don't encourage browsing here," he said, descending a circular iron staircase that wound up in the center of the main floor of the store.

Once he'd reached ground level, he wasn't quite as tall as he'd looked on his perch, but he was still one scary-looking guy—long, oily, raven black hair, a mustache that drooped around the sides of his mouth, and full lips in a perpetual pout.

"Why don't we just cut to the chase, then?" he said when he'd come over to where Megan was standing. "Why don't you tell me what it is specifically that you're interested in? Satanic cults? Grave robbing? Descriptions of exactly how bad a ghoul's breath is?"

She had to laugh at this last. "Oh no," she protested. "Nothing that specialized. I'm only . . . it's just . . . well, you see I have this friend and she thinks some of her friends might be a little . . . well . . . Undead."

"Undead?" he said. "Ah. Now we can get down to brass tacks. Vampires? Revenants? Zombies?"

She exhaled with relief. He wasn't going to be shocked, or even skeptical. Of course not. This was simply business as usual to him. It was as though she'd come into a tie shop and he'd asked her if she was interested in stripes or dots.

"Well, I . . . I mean she . . . hasn't seen any bats or coffins around, so I . . . she . . . thinks probably . . . revenants."

He strode toward the staircase and began to climb. He moved his massive bulk smoothly. The store was air conditioned to superchill and over his suit he was wearing a flowing black coat that swooshed when he walked. When he'd been a few minutes scanning one of the uppermost shelves, he began pulling books off it, piling them in an unwieldy stack he then careened back down with.

"Here you go, everything you could want to know about the Undead. Maybe *more* than you want to know."

"Uh . . . Mr. . . . ."

"Levant. Lucien Levant."

"Mr. Levant. I haven't got the money to buy any of these books."

He waved a hand at her.

"Of course not! What do you think I am? I've been in this business for thirty years. I can tell in an instant the browser from the earnest seeker from the emergency case. Which is to say, *you*. Emergency cases don't get charged. Goodness, can you imagine the bad karma I'd get if I let a customer pay for a book on vampires when her neck was up against the fangs? No, no, my dear. Just sit down in the back and read to your heart's content. I'll bring you a cup of tea while you work."

Megan sat down at a small, rickety table against the back wall, pulled out her notepad and pen, and opened the first book, scanning the pages until she came to something that seemed to apply. She started to write:

> The revenant has typically died a violent death. Often, his body was never found or properly put to rest through burial. And so the soul reenters its former physical form, restless and agitated because it is past its natural life, but unable to cross over into the peacefulness of death.

Mr. Levant brought her the cup of tea. She went on to the next volume.

> It is not difficult to identify revenants. They are seldom seen in the daylight, and have an aversion to the sun. They cast no shadows, have no reflections in mirrors, and are unphotographable. They do not eat. Black is their signature color.

Megan stopped to think. Black was certainly their signature color. And it was definitely true that you hardly ever saw anyone from The Band until late afternoon, and even then they usually stayed behind the tinted glass of their cars. And this could explain why Natalie and Laura hadn't wanted to come into the fitting room with her and deal with all those mirrors. And only now did she realize what was different about their party—there'd been no food. Not so much as a single potato chip.

She went on to a small volume, bound in purple leather.

*   *   *

The Undead may spend thousands of years playing out their half-lives, but they remain eternally fixated on the period of their resolved deaths.

When she finished the last of the books, she closed it and looked up to see Lucien Levant.

"Find what you need to get out of your fix?"

"What makes you think I'm . . . er, my friend . . . is in a fix?"

"Please. Anyone whose social circle includes members of the shall we say . . ."

"Undead?"

"Precisely. yes, I'd say those unlucky persons with such nefarious social acquaintances are, by definition, in a fix."

"Why?"

"Because the Undead enjoy company. They like to expand their ranks. They are always on the prowl for something—or someone—fresh. And if I might hazard a guess, it is you—or as you so quaintly put it, your friend—who is the tasty morsel they're eyeing at the moment."

"But how will they get her . . . oh, all right—*me?*"

Suddenly, Levant lost his supercilious tone and grew dead serious. "The one thing you must never do, never—which is to say *not ever*—is to let yourself fall asleep in their presence."

"Why not?"

"Oh, come now. Take a little guess."

"Because that's when they get me at my most vulnerable and put me under their spell?"

"Right you are. But it starts before that. First you get lazy and off your guard around them. Their peculiarities seem less and less peculiar to you. You are lulled into thinking they are your friends and your destiny is inextricably tied up with them."

As he was talking, Megan was partially identifying herself, but the symptoms and signs Levant was describing absolutely and dead-on accurately applied to someone else—Toby. He was already in the process of being taken over by them. She'd bet anything the initiation next weekend involved sleeping in the cave, something like that, something overnight that would end for Toby with a dawn in which he woke to find himself a cute, funny, hunky, regular teenage guy. Who also just happened to be a pet of the Undead.

9

Although the bus hummed along the highway on the way back, outdoor scenes passing behind green glass, Megan didn't fall asleep as she had on the way to the city. She was too agitated now, thinking about The Band, about Toby. About Iris and how Megan had brushed her off when she'd only been trying to help. About her mom, whose suspicions about The Band seemed mild now in the face of what was becoming the all-too-clear truth about them.

She felt suddenly in the middle of a nightmare with no way out. All of this seemed much too big and complicated for her to solve alone. She took out her notepad and began a list of everything she'd found out, all the information on The Band that she'd gathered, and tried to put the pieces together.

Something kept sticking in her mind. One of the books had mentioned the Undead fixating on the period around their death. Maybe there was some connection between this and the way The Band loved old music. Not *that* old. They didn't long for Mozart, so they apparently hadn't been undead all that long. When she scanned her memory, it seemed to Megan that the music they liked was from about when her own parents had been in high school. Maybe twenty years back or so.

Suddenly she remembered the time they'd run into Shane and Laura at the mall, how her mother thought she'd been on a date with him. Maybe she had! Megan felt a shudder pass through her.

The return route the bus took was different from the way Megan had gone into the city. After the umpteenth stop at a gas station or behind a church in this or that small town, she realized she'd gone on an express and was heading home on a local.

The next stop was the first one out of the mountains, back into the desert. As the bus pulled off the highway, she saw a sign at the side of the road: ARLENE—POP. 168. A feeling rushed through her, as though she was standing in the dark and something furry had brushed up against her.

The town had obviously seen better days. Stores on the side streets were mostly boarded up, leaving a main street about two blocks long—a grocery, some sort of government-looking building, two taverns, and a hardware store. The bus pulled up with a sigh of air brakes in front of an old café—Al's Kitchen—and the passenger door by the driver hissed open. On the way out, the driver had been a man, but this one was a woman. Megan rushed up to her.

"How long does the bus stop here?"

The driver—whose name tag said she was Gwen—smiled and said, "As long as it takes me to get a cup of Al's java, and use the little girls' room."

"Oh," Megan said. That wouldn't give her enough time to do any exploring. "Well, then, is there another bus coming through that goes to Blue Mesa?"

The driver pulled out a well-folded and refolded schedule.

"Yep. Another local should be along about 3:45."

Megan looked at her watch. That gave her nearly an hour and a half.

"In that case, I think I might stick around a bit and see the local sights."

The driver looked at her as though she'd just escaped from an asylum, but only said, "To each her own. Just make sure you don't leave anything behind in your seat."

Megan had a piece of pie at Al's. The sign said "homemade," but she doubted anyone could make pie this bad at home. As she was paying up, she asked Al, on a hunch, "Is there a town cemetery nearby?"

He looked at her suspiciously. What did he think— that she was a teenage grave robber?

"My great-aunt used to live here, and I think she's buried in town," she improvised. "I wanted to pay my respects."

"What was her name?"

"Abigail Smith," Megan said, figuring there had to be at least one Smith in any cemetery. At any rate, it seemed to satisfy Al.

He nodded and rubbed his whiskey chin and pointed out the window. "Take a right when you get out of here and walk about a mile. Just past the Serpentarium . . ."

"The what?!"

"Don't worry. Not much of a tourist attraction. People didn't want to pay good money to see snakes, I guess. Anyway, it's been boarded up for years. There probably aren't many snakes still living in there 'cept a couple of old cobras."

She couldn't tell if he was serious or just teasing her.

"Just step lively as you go by. On the left, you'll see a church and a sign for the cemetery up behind it on a little hill. That's where you'll find your Aunt Abigail."

"Thanks," she said, paying hurriedly. She needed to get out before Al started asking questions about dear old Aunt Abby.

The sun was treacherous as she followed the road out of town. She pulled the bill of her baseball cap around from back to front to give her eyes some shade, took off the old shirt of her dad's she was wearing over her tank top, and tied its arms around her waist.

When she got to the Serpentarium, she stayed as far across the road as she could get while still staying on the gravel shoulder and out of the tall weeds, which looked like extremely likely cobra hangouts.

She walked past the church, which had had a coat of white paint at one time, but was now mostly rotten boards with flaking-off paint. She walked up the small hill beyond the church, and there was the little cemetery, just as Al had said. A few Joshua trees here and there gave some shade, but beyond that this was a place that belonged to the desert and those who had died there.

She walked aimlessly among the tombstones. Well, not quite aimlessly, but she couldn't exactly say what she was looking for, either. One of the first names she noticed was Abigail Smith.

"My dear aunt," she said aloud and couldn't suppress a laugh, even though it was a pretty ghoulish joke. It was in the middle of laughing that her eye caught the name on the next stone over, and her laugh died in her throat:

MARNIE SLADE
BELOVED DAUGHTER, SISTER, FRIEND
1957–1972

Wasn't Marnie the name of the friend Laura thought she looked so much like? The friend they'd "lost touch with"?

"Right," she said aloud to herself. "It's kind of easy to lose touch with people when they're dead."

She looked at the next grave marker. It belonged to Curt Heflin, a loving son, who also died in 1972, in his teens.

There were more, a whole row of markers. All teenagers who died in 1972. Then, at the very end of the row was a larger marker, maybe five feet high, carved out of black granite. Carved into it were the words:

OUR LOVED ONES WHO ARE MISSING

As she read down the list of names, she felt like someone was slamming her up against a wall of cold steel.

SHANE CONROY
BELOVED SON
1956–1972

LAURA HUNTER
SHE WILL ALWAYS BE MISSED
1957–1972

They were all there. Natalie. Joey. James. All of them died in 1972, presumably with the others, but they were set apart. Missing. Missing from what? Then it hit her. It must have been an accident of some sort. The others had all been found, but Shane, Laura, Natalie, James, and Joey's bodies had been missing. That's why there were no grave markers for them, only this group memorial. That's why they were still on earth, restlessly roaming the desert while their friends were at peace. The puzzle was beginning to come together.

All of a sudden, the afternoon turned black and cold, as though a storm was coming up. Megan put her shirt on and buttoned the cuffs against this freakishly sudden chill. But when she looked up, she saw there were no clouds overhead. This patch of darkness and whipping winds surrounded only her. A few feet off, the day was still sunny. She was being chased, captured, enclosed by fierce shadows.

Without stopping to wonder what this peculiar weather meant, Megan grabbed her knapsack and ran faster than she ever had in her life, all the way to the town limits sign.

Out of breath and on her way back to the café, Megan almost missed a second-story window above the hardware store, with lettering identifying the offices of the *Arlene Sentinel*.

I'll bet they have files going back to 1972, she thought as she found the entrance. She looked over her shoulder before going in, to see if any shadows were on her tail. She would have rather just headed straight for the next bus and gotten out of here, but she felt she was really close now to discovering the whole story of The Band. She didn't want to give up until she got it.

At first she thought the office was closed, but when

she peered through the glass door she could see a light on over a desk off to the side. She pushed against the door and walked in.

"Can I help you?" called out a voice, followed by a young woman not much older than Megan. She was short and plump and had a friendly, open look to her that made it easy for Megan to tell her what she needed.

"I'm looking for your back files from 1972," she said.

The woman nodded. "We go all the way back to 1897," she said. "Of course, it's all on microfilm. Do you know how to use a machine?"

Megan shook her head.

"Come on, then. I'll show you. What week do you want?"

Megan had to answer in the negative again. "That's the thing. I don't really know. Something bad happened. Lots of high school kids got killed."

"Oh. You want to know about the band bus crash."

"What?!" Did this pleasant woman in this nice office already know about The Band?

"Yes. The Arlene High School marching band was on its way back from Palm Corners, where the team had just won a big game. It was late October, which is our brief rainy season here, and they were coming through the mountains and something happened. Nobody knows to this day what exactly went wrong. A skid probably. Anyway, the bus careened off the road, into the canyon below. It was horrible. Eighteen dead, as I recall. Most of their families moved away afterward. Couldn't stand being around all the reminders, I guess. But here,"—she held out a roll of microfilm to Megan—"you can read all about it for yourself."

She set Megan up at the machine and located the correct roll. After a bit of whirring through earlier issues Megan found herself looking at huge black and white letters:

AHS BAND BUS CRASHES
ON WAY HOME FROM GAME
18 Dead, No Survivors

Megan read on: " . . . through a guard rail . . . crossing San Gabriels . . . five bodies not recovered . . . probably lost in the explosion . . ."

And then their names, the names of her friends Laura and Shane. Natalie. James. Joey.

She knew what all this meant, but somehow it still wouldn't come together in a way that made sense. Everything was there in Lucien Levant's books and yet her mind couldn't accept it. The thing was, if they were really dead, how could she have been at a party with them last weekend?

Suddenly she felt a hand on her shoulder and she jumped about three inches out of the chair.

"Oh, I'm sorry," said the newspaper woman. "I didn't mean to startle you, but I need to close up now."

"It's okay," Megan said, putting her hand over her heart, feeling it thumping against her palm. "I guess I was pretty deep in there."

"Did you get what you want?"

"I got what I needed, thanks," Megan said. "Which, in this case, is different from what I want."

By the time she came out of the *Sentinel*'s offices, it was after 4:30. The bus she'd been planning to catch was at 3:45, and even with that she would have been late. Her parents were expecting her back on the one that arrived in Blue Mesa at 3:00.

85

She ran across to the café, hoping she hadn't missed the last bus of the day, hoping Al had a pay phone. It was bad enough that she was going to be in deep trouble back home. She didn't want to add to it spending a night alone in Arlene, with her shadowy friends from the graveyard.

10

Al's Café had closed for the day by the time Megan got there. Actually, the whole town looked as though it had shut down. There were no cars parked on the main street, no other people in sight.

She looked longingly through the front window of the café at the pay phone hanging on the wall. Why hadn't she thought to call home earlier—from here, or while she was at the newspaper? By now her father would be going ballistic. Her mother would probably have already had a heart attack.

She looked around and sighed with relief. She could see from where she stood that the gas station across the street had a pay phone hanging outside. She ran across, and in her excitement, didn't realize until she heard the distinct absence of a dial tone that she was holding a receiver attached to a wire cord, but that the cord was completely pulled out of the phone. Then she noticed the penciled Out of Order sign taped to the dial.

"Argh," she groaned heading back to the café. The bus schedule was posted in the window and— lucky break—there was another due through in about twenty minutes. There was nothing to do now but sit and wait on the narrow bench on the front porch of the café.

She was so anxious about how worried her parents would be and how much trouble she was going to be in, that at first she didn't notice that the silence of the sleepy main street was gradually being broken by strains of music. She couldn't imagine where it was coming from and opened her backpack to see if her Walkman had somehow turned itself on. But no, it was off.

Even as she zipped her backpack shut, the music was becoming louder and clearer. It was an oldie her dad loved—James Taylor's "Fire and Rain," but underlaid with a rumbling sound that was distinctly not the throbbing of guitar strings. More like the slow roll of old car engines.

And then there were the cars themselves cruising slowly out of town, following each other in a black parade, a procession with funereal overtones. The Camaro was in the lead, followed by the Corvette, and then by Joey's old bomb of a Ford.

Megan's heart took a leap. What was The Band doing here? How had they found her out? Why were they coming after her?

And then she realized they weren't here because of her. They were in Arlene because this was their home. Real life might have moved on and their families might have moved away, but their friends were still out at the town cemetery, where a resting place awaited them, too. If they no longer had a home, this was probably the closest they were going to get.

She couldn't tell if they saw her. She was in the shadows now that the afternoon had grown late. She held her breath in case her slightest movement might attract their attention. When they cruised past, out of town, she exhaled and began shivering, in spite of it being about 85 degrees out.

They had come from the direction of the cemetery. Did they sleep there during the day, like vampires? Was it *their* shadows that had passed over her as she stood among the headstones? Had they seen her looking for them? Did they know how much she now knew of their horrible secret?

She waited, breathing shallowly, to see if they'd come back, but once they'd gone there was only the deadly stillness, broken occasionally by the mournful cry of crows alighting on the phone lines.

When the bus finally wheezed up in front of the café, and the driver—this time it was a young guy—opened the door to her, Megan felt so relieved to see another human that tears inadvertently began rushing down her cheeks.

"Hey, you okay?" he asked, looking around to see if anything was wrong.

"Yeah," she said, wiping her eyes with her wrist. "I'm fine, really."

"You don't look fine, he said. "You look like you just saw a ghost."

She knew her parents would be freaked out, but still she was surprised to see them standing there, waiting for her behind the post office. They were so happy to see her, they didn't even seem angry.

"Oh, honey!" her mother said, pulling her into a crushing hug.

"Megan, where have you *been?!*" her dad asked. Abe was sitting on his shoulders, happy in his own little way, shouting "Mepo! Mepo!" which was his name for her.

She was incredibly happy to see them, too. And

sorry she'd gotten everybody so upset, and she told them so. Fortunately, she'd had the whole bus ride in to come up with a plausible cover story.

"It was awful. I just got so horribly lost," she started.

"I thought you were going to take a cab," her mother said.

"I did on the way to the music shop, but then I couldn't find one on the way back, and so I started walking and that's when I got lost."

From there she launched into a supercomplicated story of stopping in at a coffee shop, using the restroom, locking herself in, the lock breaking, the management calling a locksmith, then finally getting a taxi, which then got a flat tire. When she was finished, her parents were looking at her with wide eyes, but she couldn't tell whether they were wide with amazement or disbelief.

"That's quite a story," her dad said. He put Abe down and took off his baseball cap, running a hand through his hair as if stalling for time to decide whether her account had any ring of truth to it.

"Wasn't there any point at which you could've called?" asked her mother.

"Honestly, there just wasn't. By the time I finally got to the bus station, the next one was just about to leave and I didn't want to miss it, so I just kept running toward the gate."

She saw her parents exchange a look, then shrug.

"We were pretty worried," her dad said. "We like to think that at sixteen we can trust you out on your own."

"Maybe next time you need some more of those reeds," her mother mused, "I'll just run you in myself."

"Yeah, well, I got enough to last a while," Megan said, pulling out of her knapsack the bag of reeds she'd put in before she left. Inside she let out a whistle of happiness that she'd gotten away with her lie. She'd had to tell it. They wouldn't have believed the truth. If she'd told them what had really happened—what was really *happening*—they'd probably, think she was crazy. At the very least they'd think she was lying and ground her. And she couldn't be grounded now. Not if she was going to save Toby.

Megan's parents let her off the hook for being so late coming back from L.A., but they weren't totally satisfied with her story, she could tell. For the past couple of years, they hadn't really questioned her judgment about friends and boyfriends and where she went, but now they wanted an accounting of where she was going and whom she was spending her time with. They wanted to meet all her new friends.

Luckily, she hadn't heard from The Band in a few days. She didn't want to have to deal with them anyway, let alone have them over for a little tea party with her mom and dad. ("Don't you want any snacks?" "How peculiar—you're sitting right in front of this mirror, but I can't see your reflections.")

Actually, her mother had run into Shane on her own. At the K-Mart.

"I was looking for a welcome mat for the front door," she told Megan when she got back, "and he was at the other end of the aisle in Housewares, buying candles. *Lots* of candles."

"Oh," Megan said, hoping this was the end of her mother's story, but suspecting it wasn't.

"He tried to act as though he didn't recognize me, but I could tell he did."

"Oh, Mom." Megan could just see the rest coming.

"So I went over and said hello and reintroduced myself. He said hi, but turned so I couldn't get a really good look at him. I told him he certainly was the spitting image of his father. At first he didn't seem to know what I was taking about. I told him we'd been on a date once, a million years ago, just before my family moved away from here."

"What'd he say?"

"Not much. Just that he wouldn't know anything about that. He and his dad hadn't ever been close and he hadn't seen him for some time. At first I thought it was just that I was boring him with some ancient history, but he wasn't bored, he was seriously nervous."

"Maybe he's just shy."

"Maybe. But when he would look at me—which he only did in these tiny flickers—I could tell he recognized me, and not just from the other day at the mall."

"What are you talking about?"

Her mother paused for a long moment. "I don't know. Something's fishy here, but I can't find the fish. Just what is going on with him and his motley crew of friends?"

"I don't know," Megan lied. "They're just sort of different is all."

"I've never forbidden you to have any friends you wanted, but . . ."

"Don't worry," Megan said. "I've already decided I don't want to hang with them anymore."

"Can you tell me why?"

Megan paused and thought what a relief it would be to just spill everything to her mother. But then she realized there was no way her mother would believe her story. She was having a hard time believing it herself.

"They smoke," she said. "And they don't use their seat belts."

So The Band escaped having to pass parental muster, but when Toby called Wednesday night and asked Megan if she wanted to go to the library on a study date, she had to tell him, "You'll have to go through the court-martial, I'm afraid. Firing squad if my parents don't like you."

"It's okay. Parents usually find me adorable. It's my boy-next-door good looks."

She was really happy he'd called. She'd been worried he wouldn't want anything to do with her since she'd brought up her doubts about The Band. They hadn't really talked since then and as far as she knew he was still going through with the initiation. She had to come up with a way to wrest him out of their clutches, but clearly the direct approach was not going to work. He was so in thrall to them that he'd never believe anything bad about them, no matter what proof she came up with.

It went fine between him and her parents. It was easy introducing them to someone who wasn't Undead—at least not yet. He and her dad followed all the same sports teams, and her mother later told Megan she thought he was a hunk.

Sitting around, having a Coke with them, it almost seemed for a brief moment that they were normal kids having a normal date. But then Megan snapped back to reality. This was Wednesday night. Laura had said they were going to initiate Toby on Friday, when the moon turned full.

"Toby," she said when they were in his car on the way to the library, "where's this cave where they're having your initiation?" She tried to make her voice sound interested, but only in an offhand way.

"Why do you care?" he said. "I thought you were sure The Band was a bunch of werewolves or something."

"Yeah," she said, faking a laugh. "Werewolves of London. I know, I get these goofy ideas sometimes." She didn't want him to get his guard up against her. If she couldn't count on him to cooperate, at least she could try to get information from him. "But really, you're my favorite werewolf in town. So tell me where they're giving you your honorary fangs."

"Well," he said, making a gesture of combing the hair on his face back with his claws, "actually, it's going to be out at this trendy, happening little cave."

"In the desert?"

"Yeah, about a mile beyond the Blue Mesa. Native American tribal peoples used it before The Band did. They left drawings on the walls. It's a cool place. It should be a cool ceremony. I asked them if you could come, but they were kind of odd about it. I guess they don't want any outsiders."

Or anybody who's on to them, Megan thought. She'd been invited before, by Natalie and Laura at the mall. Now apparently she'd been uninvited. Clearly they didn't want anyone throwing a monkey wrench in the works. So it looked as though she was going to have to crash the party.

Iris was waiting for her in the cafeteria at lunchtime. "Waiting" as in "ambush."

"So what's happening?" she said, elbowing Megan in the salad bar line.

"Oh, nothing much."

"I heard you got lost big-time in L.A."

"How'd you hear about that?"

"Give me a break. Your parents practically had a four-state alert out. They were printing up the milk carton with your picture on it. So of course they came over to see if you were hanging out at my place." She took a breath before adding, "I told them I doubted you were really going into the city to buy clarinet reeds since I'd just seen you pull a fistful out of your knapsack the other day."

"You didn't!"

"Of course, I didn't. I'm your friend. Even if you're not mine. Even if you shut me out."

Megan didn't say anything, just kept picking at her chef's salad.

"Even if you go all the way to L.A. on some big secret mission and don't let me in on what it is," Iris tried again.

Megan looked across the table at Iris, her "Iris" barrettes sticking out from the sides of her hair, slices of banana sticking out the sides of her peanut butter and banana and potato chip sandwich. She looked about twelve years old. Megan felt about forty-five, as though in these past few weeks she had aged thirty years, had accumulated the weight of a world of terrible knowledge she now wished she didn't have. She wished she could go back to being as innocent as Iris. And she just couldn't bring her into all of this. She was safely on the outside, a curious observer of extraterrestrials. But Megan now knew these aliens among them were dangerous. Somehow she had to keep them from taking Toby along, getting him under their control. They weren't going to like her meddling with their plans, and who knew what they would do to her when they saw that Megan had not only left the fold, but had turned against them?

She felt as though she was entering a dark place filled with death and danger. How could she bring someone into it who was wearing barrettes? And so she lied to the one person she could have counted on to help her fight The Band.

"Iris, I went to a doctor. To get birth control pills."

"You mean . . . well . . . you and Toby?!"

"Not yet. But we do seem to be getting serious and I want to be prepared in case."

"Oh. Well, that sounds smart, I guess. I'm sorry. I didn't mean to pry into your personal stuff. I thought it was something to do with The Band. I had a nightmare last night about you and them. In a cave."

Megan didn't ask for details.

12

Thursday night Megan was home working on her Social Studies project—gathering six versions of the same news story from various papers and magazines to show their differences in approach and coverage. She'd had this great idea of including videos of the story as done by two of the L.A. TV stations. She was trying to set up the VCR so it would be ready to go when her story—a grisly murder in a fast food restaurant—came on.

Abe was bugging her like crazy. He should really have been in bed, but he'd woken up with a bad dream and their father said he could stay up a while, until he'd forgotten the monsters.

"I help," he told Megan with confidence as he grabbed the remote control out of her hand.

"No, you do *not* help," she informed him. "The very best I can hope is that you don't hinder." She yanked the remote back from him; of course, he immediately began crying.

"What's going on?" their dad shouted from the basement, where he was working in his shop. He took old wooden chairs and tables he picked up at flea markets and painted them in wild, new wavy color patterns, then sold them at about five times the price he'd bought them for. He was very artistic; everyone wanted his stuff. He was getting to the point where he was making almost as much money from his hobby as he was from his regular jobs.

Abe, seeing that he was getting some attention, turned his crying into wailing.

"What the . . . ?" Megan heard, followed by her dad's footsteps thudding up the basement stairs, followed by her dad in the flesh, irritated at having been interrupted.

Megan explained what was going on.

"Tell you what," her dad said. "Why don't you two take a break from each other? You can go get us some ice cream at the 7-Eleven. I'll watch Abe and tape your news show."

"I just want the one segment."

"I'm sure I'll be able to handle it, technologically speaking," her father teased, grabbing the remote from her and flopping onto the sofa. "This is one job my years as a couch potato has prepared me for."

Megan took the five dollars her dad gave her, along with the keys to his car, and headed out to the 7-Eleven. As she drove she thought about how to crash The Band's initiation ceremony and somehow sabotage it. She didn't have anything firm in mind beyond waiting in the parking lot of the Tumbleweed Drive-In and following them to the cave when they picked Toby up.

As she drove she pushed the buttons on the car radio, scanning for a song she liked. On one station she heard the disk jockey saying, "Tonight's the night to get out and howl, my friends. The full moon is upon us."

She looked up at the night sky, which was dazzling out here in the desert, the stars so brilliant, and there it was—a full moon. She made a fist with one hand and hit the steering wheel. She'd been tricked; the initiation wasn't tomorrow night, it was going on *right now*!

She skidded off onto the shoulder and braked the car. She put her forehead against the top of the steering wheel to try to think. The smart thing would be to continue to the 7-Eleven, get some ice cream, and go home. Her dad would be expecting her back soon. Besides, she might already be too late. Toby was probably theirs by now.

The mere thought of this—of someone terrific like Toby turned into some kind of zombie by these creeps—made her so angry it blotted out all her sensible thinking on the subject. She spun around and headed in the opposite direction, toward the caves past the Blue Mesa. She tried to keep from speeding; she really couldn't afford to get pulled over.

When she got to the mesa, she shot off the road and across the desert, kicking up sand with her spinning tires as she headed for the caves. Soon she was surrounded by an odd darkness. The moon threw a strange light on everything—like infrared, only white. Infrawhite.

The caves, when she reached them, were bathed in this color; it made them look like soft igloos, or the tents of Martian hunters. It was a landscape of some other planet, not Earth.

At first she couldn't see any signs of life other than desert creatures—lizards and small mice—skittering out of the way of her headlights. But then, as she crept along, she began to see a wavering light coming from one of the caves farther up. She cut off her lights so she wouldn't be seen and slowed the car to a crawl.

She turned off the air conditioning and rolled down the window. She almost knew what to expect, and sure enough there it was, rolling across the desert— James Taylor's "Fire and Rain" again, one of The Band's favorite songs.

She stopped the car and turned off the ignition. Desert creatures or not, she was going to have to go the rest of the way on foot, or risk The Band spotting her before she was ready.

She wished she were wearing clothes that were more protective. She felt vulnerable in just her old baggy shorts and a T-shirt. Luckily she had on her running shoes. If she needed to get away in a hurry, she was faster than any of the others, on foot at least.

As she approached the glowing cave, she could see the muted, flickering light coming from inside, but couldn't see what was creating it. Then someone came out. Natalie. She was dressed in black, but different from how Megan had ever seen her before, in a long black robe. As Megan approached stealthily, she could see Nat had flowers pinned in her hair. White orchids.

Then James followed her. He was wearing a similar black robe with a white orchid pinned to the collar. Megan watched as the two of them conferred in voices too low to overhear, then disappeared back into the cave. Megan decided to make her approach.

She scuttled across the sand as fast as she could, tripping once on a rock. She twisted her ankle, but she didn't have time to think about it; she just picked herself up and ran painfully the rest of the way. When she got to the caves, which were hollowed out of the side of a huge, high rock formation, she pressed herself against the sloping wall of rock and moved slowly toward the glowing opening. When she finally got there, she stopped for a moment to prepare herself for whatever strange sight would greet her when she looked in.

Everyone was there. Shane. Laura. James and Natalie. Joey. All dressed in the same long black robes, all with white orchids either pinned to their collars or in their hair, or in loose leis around their necks. Like Natalie, they looked different from how she'd ever seen them before. She could barely recognize them; they were such ghoulish caricatures of themselves. Their skin was pale and bloodless and seemed to hang from their faces loosely. Their eyes were sunken and bloodshot, their hair thin and limp. It was as if they'd aged but simultaneously stayed the same, as if they were weary, but unable to sleep. These were not the cool kids she'd been dying to get in with. Now, in what she guessed was their truest form, they looked like derelicts, transients, persons with no home, no place to rest. They were both unbearably sad to look at, and creepily frightening.

The glow from the cave, she could now see, was the emanation of hundreds of candles. Black candles, set on every horizontal surface from the floor up to the highest rock shelves in the cave. Here and there among these were incense burners smoking upward with a thick, flowery fragrance that overwhelmed Megan with a sudden memory of her grandmother's funeral.

There was no dead body at this ceremony, though—only a sleeping one. Toby. He was stretched out in the center of the cave on a raised platform of rock. She wondered if the early tribes that had inhabited this land had used this as an altar. It was as though history had gone into a warp. Here they were near the end of the twentieth century, and a human sacrifice of sorts was being made on this ancient altar.

Toby looked asleep, resting peacefully. There was an open vial of a dark purple liquid on the platform next to him, making Megan suspect he'd been drugged. Next to the bottle, even more ominously, was a small dagger with a jeweled blue handle.

The others were gathered around him, their arms linked with each other's, swaying back and forth to "Fire and Rain," which seemed to be repeating itself endlessly on the tape deck propped against the wall.

Megan watched as Laura stepped forward and up onto a step at the base of the platform. She was carrying a black cloth, a shroud of sorts, and unfolded it, placing it over Toby.

"Now we must wait for the Midnight Exchange, then for the night to do its part," she said, turning to the others, her eyes staring off into the middle distance, unseeing, her voice dull as clay. "If we keep our vigil, by morning he will be under our wing, to make up our number again and be released from this long time of wandering."

"No!" Megan heard herself shout, surprising herself as much the others. They all turned at once, looking at her stunned, like rabbits caught in the headlights of an approaching car.

Shane was the first to shake himself free of the mood of the ceremony and respond to the intrusion.

"Megan," he said in a voice that was unnaturally calm. "We're sorry we couldn't invite you tonight, but you see, this is a private ceremony. There's no place for outsiders, I'm afraid. And an outsider is apparently what you are."

"You've made that eminently clear with all your little research missions," Laura backed him up coolly. "Trying to find out all our secrets. Oh, Megan, don't you know we would have told you ourselves? Just like we're going to tell Toby as soon as he wakes up?"

"You mean when it's too late for him to make any decisions," Megan said, taking a step closer, now inside the cave. "When you'll have him under your spell, a slave for you to rule."

"You're looking at it all wrong," Shane said. "He'll feel fortunate, having been chosen. We choose so few."

"Yeah," Jenny Gonzales piped up in a zoned-out voice. Megan hadn't even noticed her, sitting over in a corner of the cave. "It's cool afterward. None of the old problems and decisions. You just do as you're told and everything's okay."

"Oh, that sounds great, all right. Like being a prisoner without bars."

"Could this be sour grapes, perhaps," James said, "because we didn't choose *you*?"

"If you didn't choose me, it was because I was on to you and you knew it," Meg challenged.

"Yes," Laura said witheringly, "the little detective. We were quaking in our boots when you found the cemetery."

"Well, I *could* tell someone everything I know," Megan threatened. "Someone like the police."

"Oh, boy," Joey said with a fake tremor in his voice. "That would be really scary. For sure they'd believe you, and then they'd rush out to arrest us for assault with intent to burglarize souls. And then what are they going to do—give us the death sentence? Give me a break."

Megan silently conceded the point—what could she tell anyone that wouldn't sound fantastic? And what human punishments could be inflicted on The Band?

She looked over at Toby again and asked the question she'd been both preoccupied with and avoiding. "What's the dagger for?"

"Oh, Megan," Shane said, "we thought you'd been doing your homework. We'll have to give you a D on the pop quiz for missing this one."

"Blood exchange," Laura said, as though stating the boringly obvious. "We take a bit of his, give him some of ours." At this, Shane pricked up his thumb with the tip of the knife, eliciting a thin trickle of blood. Megan had to suppress a gasp when she saw that it was blue. She stared in fear and wonder, but no one else seemed to find it in the least unusual.

"It's a little gross," Natalie added, "but it's the only way, really. I mean, we didn't make up the rules; they're part of the deal."

"Look," Shane said, coming over and putting an arm around Megan, making her shiver as if the temperature had suddenly dropped fifty degrees. "I understand your concern. You like Toby. But we *need* him. If we can fill in our ranks with—well, with volunteers—back to our original number, we can be freed from this."

"But why do you need to be freed? Why can't you just keep going along like this?" Megan asked, seeing a tiny crack in their wall, thinking maybe she could talk them out of taking Toby.

"Megan, you like being a high school junior," Laura said. "But how would you like it for the next twenty years? We've been wandering out there"—she pointed upward—"for some time. And now we've been allowed back here to get it right this time."

"Get *what* right?" Megan said, but no one was answering her question directly.

"If all goes well, we'll all be released," Shane said.

"Released into . . . ?"

"Peace," Laura said.

"Peace for you," Megan said, hearing her voice rise, "but you've already died. Toby's still alive. Are you thinking of taking him along? Or Jenny? Or the others you're recruiting?"

James shrugged. "Some sacrifices will have to be made. That's always the case with worthy causes."

"You creeps," Megan said. "I don't know why I ever thought I could reason with you. I'm acting like you're regular people. Like you're my friends. But you're not. You're not even human."

"We like to think of ourselves as *para*-human," James said.

Megan looked around, sickened that she'd even tried to reason with The Band.

"Look, I'm leaving. And I'm taking Toby with me," she said with a confidence she didn't feel, wresting herself free from Shane's chilling embrace and leaping onto the steps that led to the platform. Immediately, the others sprang up at once and grabbed her, pulling her to the ground. Shane was leaning over her with the jeweled dagger in his hand, and pressed against her throat.

"Don't even think you can stand in our way."

Megan shuddered at the ice cold steel of the knife blade held against her skin. *I'm going to die,* she thought, and somehow that awful knowledge made her more angry than afraid.

"You're not going to be able to pull this off," Megan said.

"Oh, but we *can*," Laura said. "That's the beauty of it. We can do whatever we want. In this desert we're like the old joke about the 500-pound gorilla." As Laura hunched over her, Megan could see in the flickering candlelight what the long years of being Undead had wrought, in the lines and sagging of Laura's face and the yellowing of her teeth.

"If you can't beat us," Shane whispered, so close to her face she could feel his warm breath, "why not join us? Even though you've been faithless, we'd forgive you. Come on. Leave your boring little life behind. Travel with us—in style, over to the other side."

The knife wavered a little in his hand. *He doesn't want to kill me*, Megan realized, and with that thought came hope. She might not be able to rescue Toby, but if she could escape with her own life, maybe she could get another chance. She needed to buy herself some time.

"I'm sorry guys, but this isn't my thing. I *like* my boring little existence. But if it's what Toby wants, I won't stand in his way. Just let me go and you can get back to your ceremony."

"Get rid of her," Laura hissed. "If she won't come to us, we have no use for her."

Megan held her breath. After what seemed like hours, she felt the knife pull back from her throat. "No," Shane said softly. "We don't have to hurt her. There's no way she can stop us. Sorry it didn't work out, Megan," he added. "You were one I especially wanted. I always felt you belonged with us, to replace Marnie." Megan could see a flash of sadness in his expression for a moment, as if he couldn't bear to lose yet another friend. Then his stare quickly turned back into ice. "Now get out of here."

She got to her feet and cast an anguished look back at the shrouded Toby.

"Don't even think about it," James said. "He stays. We don't need you, but we do need him."

"And we're not all as soft-hearted as Shane. We'll do anything to protect our interests," Natalie added, taking the knife out of Shane's hand, running a thumb along its razorlike edge.

Megan could see from the cold stares of the other Band members and the indifference in Jenny Gonzales's expression that she had no allies here, only enemies. She knew they would stop at nothing if she tried to interfere with their plans. She had no choice but to run out of the cave, into the black desert night, free herself, but leaving Toby with them.

13

Megan woke up the next morning with her heart racing. It was getting more and more difficult to separate her nightmares from the realities of her waking life. Her dreams had been murky, malevolent ones about The Band's hold on Toby, but then, so were her thoughts.

The worst thing was, she knew that to have any chance to save Toby, she had to come up with a plan soon, before The Band completed their sinister recruitment program. And Megan had been grounded for three weeks. Last night, when she'd gotten back "from the 7-Eleven" an hour and a half late with a carton of the wrong flavor ice cream, she told her parents she'd gone to three stores before giving up on finding Cherry Garcia, the family's favorite.

"How about we give you a chance to tell us where you really were," her father had said. Her mother just sat there in silence, but Megan could tell from her chewed cuticles that she'd been worried, waiting for Megan to get home.

But Megan had to stick to her story, no matter how stupid and unbelievable it was, because she couldn't come up with a better lie, and the truth would've been a thousand times worse.

She knew she needed an ally. There was no way she could stop The Band on her own, and no one she could really turn to for help. Unless . . . maybe . . . Iris.

Megan wrestled with her conscience over this. Bringing Iris in on what was happening could put her in danger. On the other hand, she was so smart and resourceful that she just might be able to come up with some way to rescue Toby, even now, and maybe put a stop to The Band. Megan herself was at a dead end. Besides, she was tired of feeling so alone in all this, and so terribly frightened.

So she skipped breakfast that morning, both to avoid her family and to be waiting on Iris's front porch when she came out. She watched her friend emerge, burdened like a pack mule under the weight of her books and lunch and microscope box.

"What're you doing here?" she said, clearly surprised to see Megan.

"I need your help."

"Okay," Iris said in a wait-and-see tone of voice.

"Can you skip school today?"

Iris stopped to think. "I don't know. I never have before. I'd blow a perfect attendance record. . . ."

"Iris. Believe me. This is bigger than a perfect attendance record."

Iris looked at her for a moment, then said, "Okay. Where are we going?"

"Los Angeles."

"What?!"

"Just walk with me downtown and I'll explain on

the way. We don't have much time. We need to catch the eight-thirty bus."

As they walked, Megan told Iris everything—all that she had found out at the bookstore, and in Arlene at the cemetery and the newspaper office. She described the frightening initiation ceremony last night.

"Have you seen Toby since?" Iris asked,

"No. I'm sure he'll be back in school today, just seeming a little more listless than usual, a little vague around the eyes—subtle changes most people won't even notice. According to that book Mr. Levant showed us, revenants can't make new revenants out of their recruits; they can only get them under their control. We're the only ones who know Toby's life is no longer his own."

"What can we do?"

"I'm not sure. I'm still hoping there's some way to reverse the damage that's been done."

"But what are we going to find out in L.A.?"

"If anyone will know what to do, it's Lucien Levant. I think we've just got to throw ourselves on his mercy and see what he can come up with."

"I can't believe all you've done without me!" Iris squawked.

"I'm sorry. I just kept getting in deeper and deeper and I didn't want to put you in any danger, and I probably shouldn't even be now. . . ."

"Nonsense," said Iris as the bus pulled up. "I'd rather risk this than risk dying of boredom, which I'm very close to, having lived sixteen years in Blue Mesa."

They got seats together in the back, away from the other passengers, so they could talk freely. Megan was so relieved to have Iris in this with her, someone

111

to spill everything out to. And someone to bounce ideas off of. Two heads would, she hoped, be better than one.

"So they've got Toby now, and Jenny Gonzales," Iris said. "They're moving toward rebuilding their school band. Who are the other kids they're trying to recruit?"

"Well, me, until last night. Ethan Hayes until he freaked out. At the party I saw Ron Mason and Antonia Greco. And they were talking about Leslie Tellman."

Iris took the names down on a sheet of loose leaf in her binder, pondered the list for a while, then said, "It looks like there's two types they're going for, musicians like you and Ethan and Toby and Leslie. The others, I don't know."

"There's something I forgot to tell you. They think I look like one of the dead kids. Marnie Somebody."

"That might be the other track then—kids who remind them of their dead friends. When they get the old school band back together, they can all finally die for real."

"Nice for the ones who are already dead," Megan said. "Not *such* a good deal for the others. We've got to do something."

Iris nodded. "We'll see what your friend at the bookstore has to say."

"I'm not surprised to see you here again," Lucien Levant said when they opened the bookstore door and the bell tinkled above their heads. They both looked up to see him leaning over the iron railing of the book loft, eyeing them.

"This is my friend, Iris Wojack. We need help. Things have gone from bad to much, much worse."

Lucien came down the steps and invited them into his reading parlor in a side room of the store.

"Let me be frank," he said. "I never like to gild the lily. You're in a tough situation. The Undead are powerful and fierce. They're desperate to get what—and who—they want, and that makes them doubly dangerous. They have nothing to lose, and they will stop at nothing. It's not good to have opponents like that."

"I see your point," Megan said. "But isn't there anything we can do?"

"First I need as much information about your Undead friends as you can give me. Every revenant has his own personality. This group may have a weak spot, a vulnerability, and we need to ferret it out."

Megan told Lucien about how Natalie and Laura had shied away from the fitting rooms. About the tombstones and the newspaper stories and what happened at the cemetery. About every detail she could remember from the initiation ceremony.

"Have you seen their blood?" he asked.

Megan nodded. "Shane cut his hand at the party." She paused.

He filled in for her. "It was blue, yes?"

Megan nodded.

"A little-known aspect of revenants," Lucien said.

"You never told me that part," Iris said, indignant.

"I didn't want to talk about it. It makes my skin crawl whenever I think about it. I also never told you that my mother once went on a date with Shane."

"The Undead are restless," Lucien said, bringing them back to the business at hand, "because some unfinished business is keeping them from dying."

"We figured that out," Megan said, "and we're

113

pretty sure Toby and the others are the replacements they need to recreate their old band. We're not quite sure how close they are to filling out the numbers."

"You remembered what I said," he glowered at her. "Never fall asleep in their presence."

"I didn't. But I think we may be a little too late for Toby," Megan said.

"Or Jenny," Iris added.

"You can still save them, but only if you can help these Undead die. Give them another chance. They're trying to get to the other side by reassembling their former number because they're lonely, but there's an easier way. They weren't supposed to die when they did. The beyond wasn't ready for them, which is why they're still roaming around causing so much trouble. But these things usually go through quite nicely on a second try. If you could recreate the circumstances of their death, give them a little push over that edge again. . . ."

"B-b-but that would be murder," Megan said.

"Oh, my dear, don't be silly," Lucien Levant said. "To kill someone, they have to be alive."

"Well, that was certainly helpful," Megan said sarcastically when they were sitting in a Chinese restaurant near the bus station. "Simply recreate the circumstances of their death," she mimicked Lucien Levant's horror-movie voice. "No problem. We just pick a rainy night and get out our bus. . . ."

"Wait a minute," Iris said, a light coming on in the back of her eyes. "The night they died was October 26. That's a week from Wednesday! Wouldn't it be much more powerful if we could make it happen then, on the anniversary of the original crash?"

"Yes!" Megan said. "Like waiting for the door to

open again and letting them go through. But how are we going to do this? I mean, it's just impossible."

"No," Iris said. "It might *just* be possible. Let's get to work!" She took out her paper and pen and began outlining a plan.

14

"Mrs. Fraser, please," Iris said boldly into the receiver. Megan sat on the top bunk in Iris's room, her feet dancing as they dangled over the edge, listening nervously to this conversation.

Iris the electronic wizard cupped her hand over the mouthpiece. "Don't worry. With this synthesizer"—she pointed at a black box leading to a wire leading to a little cap on the mouthpiece—"I can make my voice sound any way I want. In this case, I talk like this and Mrs. Fraser will hear the concerned voice of your father."

Megan flipped back against the pillows and grabbed one to smother her giggles, which she felt coming on as soon as she heard Iris say, "Yes? Mrs. Fraser? This is Steve Sanders, Megan's dad. I'm afraid our little girl is quite ill. Actually, yes, it could be quite serious. You know we recently moved here from Boulder. Well, the doctor thinks it might be a touch of Rocky Mountain Fever. Yes. Well, thanks for your concern. No, I appreciate that, but I don't think it's time just yet for a student prayer vigil."

By the time Iris was off the phone, Megan was nearly hysterical. "What are you getting me into?"

116

"Don't worry. You're very resilient. You're going to spring right back from your disease. You'll be back in school in no time. And meanwhile, we don't have to worry about you showing up for school for a few days. Now," she said, furrowing her brow, "what do you think *I'm* coming down with?"

"Too fishy," Megan said. "I think your Uncle Louie died and you have to go to the funeral. In Nebraska."

"Brilliant," Iris said, turning the dial on the synthesizer. After a few seconds, she said brightly, "Mrs. Fraser, this is Alice Wojack, Iris's mom. I'm afraid we've had a tragedy in the family. . . ."

Now they were free to work full-time on their plan, Phase 1 of which involved paying a visit to Iris's Uncle Wally, who owned an auto parts emporium.

"Basically, it's a junkyard," Iris admitted. "He takes wrecks and sells them to guys like my brother Ned, who fix them up again. Or he cannibalizes them for parts. He's had an old school bus out on the back of the lot for years. I think—even though he's notoriously stingy—we might be able to persuade him to give it to us."

The lot was a creepy place, a thousand crushed, squashed, bent, and rusted-out cars. Mangy cats darted out from under one wreck, across the dirt, and under another. Coiled on the hood of one, baking in the morning sun, was a snake. Megan hoped this would go smoothly and they wouldn't have to spend much time here.

"Now what would you girls want with a school bus?" Uncle Wally asked, chewing on a short, fat, unlit cigar.

"It's for our Homecoming parade," Iris said. "If we can get it running, we want to paint it the Mojave High School colors—tan and blue—and have our Homecoming Queen sitting on the hood."

"Well, I'd love to—you being my favorite niece and all—but as luck would have it, I've got someone interested in that bus at the moment."

"Uncle Wally," Iris said. "Come on. You know no one's been interested in that heap in all the years it's been sitting here. Who'd want their kids riding on it? If you give it to the Homecoming parade, we can put a sign on the front—DONATED BY WALLY'S AUTO EMPORIUM."

"Really?" Uncle Wally chewed the cigar some more as if still deciding, but Megan knew they had him.

They got Iris's brother Ned to tow the ramshackle bus back to town and stash it in the garage behind the sanitation plant where he worked. This was where he and his buddies tinkered with the cars they rebuilt. Megan expected they'd have to bribe and coerce him like crazy to get him to work on the bus, but apparently Ned was just devoted to Iris. As the only girl, she was the royal princess in her family. All she had to do was ask Ned and he said, "Sure."

Her brother bought the Homecoming parade ruse, just like that. Megan was amazed at what a terrific liar Iris was. She just let them roll out as though they were the truth and everyone just nodded and went along.

"You're in the major leagues of liars," she told her.

"Really. Funny, because I've never had to do it before," Iris said. "I've always been such a good child I've never needed to lie about anything. I must just be a natural."

It took Ned and his friends three days to get the bus's engine up and running.

"I still don't know how this heap is going to look in a parade," he told them, wiping a wrench on a greasy rag as he crawled out from under the bus's front end. "A fancy paint job isn't going to hide the dents, and half the windows are busted out."

"It's okay," Iris told him. "It'll still be the most original float in the parade."

Megan couldn't believe the deceitful life she was leading these days. She wasn't going to school, wasn't doing any homework, was lying to her parents about everything. She hoped she could keep it all together for a few more days, until Wednesday night.

This wasn't a certainty. Her parents were getting more and more suspicious, and she was having to take greater risks all the time. On Monday night she got caught sneaking out her bedroom window. Fortunately, the one who caught her was Abe.

"Where you go?" he said innocently.

"On an important mission," she told him, crawling back in, picking him up and sitting him on her lap on the floor. "And I'll make you a member of the secret squad if you promise not to tell Mom and Dad anything about me going out now."

He puffed out his cheeks and thought for a moment, then decided, "No, I tell them."

"You little rat," she said. He was too smart for her. She would have to resort to bribery. "All right. Don't tell and I'll get you a new Ninja Turtle."

"Two," he said, and smiled.

"All right, you little worm. Two."

He climbed down off her lap and sauntered out of the room sucking his thumb and dragging his "bankey" behind him. How could someone so little already be so successful a manipulator? Megan wondered.

At breakfast the next morning, her mother made her pancakes—a sure sign something was up. Her mother's usual swipe at making breakfast was putting a box of cold cereal on the table. If she was really bright-eyed, she'd dig out a carton of milk, too. Pancakes meant a "serious talk," which at the moment was the very last thing Megan wanted.

"Honey," her mother said as Megan poured syrup on her pancakes and tried to pretend this was a regular weekday breakfast, "your father and I are worried about you."

"Yeah?" Megan said, wondering what they'd found out. Had Mrs. Fraser called from school? Did they know she'd missed practically a week of classes? Had someone spotted her practice-driving the school bus out on the old Blue Arrow Road? Had her mom gone through her drawers and found all her notes on the Undead? Seen her taking the bus back and forth to L.A. to consult with Lucien Levant on the best methods of getting rid of a rather large group of revenants? What part of the whole terrible truth had her mother stumbled upon?

"Honey," she said, with the most sincere expression on her face. "Your dad and I think maybe you don't have enough interests, that you have too little to do with your spare time. Maybe if you took up a hobby, found a project you were interested in." She went over to the broom closet and pulled out a box and put it on the table. "Like this nice bird feeder kit."

Megan burst out laughing and couldn't stop. She was glad she had to leave "for school" and didn't have time to try to explain to her bewildered mother what was so funny.

15

"The first thing we've got to do is get hold of that purple liquid," Iris said. "The stuff you say they had at the initiation ceremony. We need The Band in their most vulnerable state, and from how you describe Toby at the ceremony, this stuff turns a person pretty near into silly putty."

"But it might not even work on the Undead. And how are we even going to find it, much less steal it?" Megan said.

"Well, we just have to hope it'll work. Where do you suppose they hang out during the day? My guess is it's somewhere around that cemetery in Arlene. And if they're good little revenants, they should be sleeping the day away, making it a piece of cake to steal anything from them."

Iris borrowed a car from Ned, who was always working on about three at a time and could usually spare one. This got them out to Arlene much faster than if they'd had to take the bus. It also felt safer to Megan. Who knew what they were going to find when they got there—and how fast they'd need to get away.

They drove past the Serpentarium.

"Boy, I wish it was still open," Iris said.

"Oh, Iris." Megan pointed toward the church. "There. Take a left up that drive."

Iris wanted to get out and see the grave markers, and when Megan showed her, she shook her head. "Wow."

"Where do you think they are?" Megan said nervously, looking around. She didn't want to stand there waiting for a tornado or monsoon or whatever other trouble The Band might stir up.

"Don't know," Iris said, peering around at things. "Close by, though. That I'm fairly sure of. Why don't we get back in the car and take a drive up that little caretaker's road?"

They wound their way along the road, which was really just a pair of parallel ruts, until they came to a little shack under a stand of trees.

"What'd I tell you?" Iris whispered, pointing to the three black cars parked in the shade.

"Maybe they use the shed as their base camp," Megan speculated.

"My thought exactly," Iris said. "Let's take a look."

They opened their car doors slowly, wincing when the rusty hinges creaked. They waited for a moment to see if the noise brought any activity from the cars.

Nothing.

They got out and walked softly over to the shed. Iris pulled on the knob and the door opened easily and soundlessly.

Inside, they had to wait a moment for their eyes to adjust to the dark. The only sunlight came through a small vent in the roof of the shack.

"Is there a light switch?" Megan asked.

123

"I don't think there's a light," Iris said, pointing toward the ceiling, from which an old, empty socket dangled. "Luckily, I brought this flash," she said, flicking it on.

"Were you a Girl Scout or something?" Megan asked. "Always prepared?"

"That's Boy Scouts, I think. And no, I'm just incredibly brilliant and well prepared all on my own." Iris ran the flashlight over the contents of the shack.

"Looks as though we've hit pay dirt," Megan said. The shed was stacked with what looked to be The Band's basic operating equipment: boxes of candles, blankets, wall pegs hung with black robes, a wine rack filled with bottles of red, and—on a high shelf in the back—a large, elaborately configured bottle of purple liquid.

"Looks like they get it in the giant economy size," Iris said. "At Revenants-R-Us."

"They won't miss a little bit," Megan said, pulling out of her back pocket an empty travel shampoo bottle.

"My, my," Iris said and whistled low. "Who's the Girl Scout?"

"Give me a lift up, will you, so I can get it off the shelf?" Megan said, using Iris's cupped hands as a stirrup, hoping against hope she wouldn't knock the bottle off the shelf. She was pretty sure the revenants *couldn't* wake up during the day, but she didn't want to take any chances.

But everything went smoothly. Megan set the bottle back exactly as she'd found it and Iris even thought to brush over their footprints with the dust and sand on the wooden floor.

Then, when they were out of the shed, nearly to their car, they heard a horrible sound—a low moan.

It didn't sound as though it was coming from the cars so much as from the ground the girls were walking on. Nor did it sound like it had been made by anything human.

They froze and stared at each other until Iris broke their paralysis. "Let's get out of here. Like now!" The old car blew exhaust out of its pipes all the way into Arlene. They couldn't see anything in the rearview mirror and finally decided no one was after them.

"Must've just been someone turning over in his grave," Iris said, but neither of them was really up to laughing at the joke.

"While you were stealing the purple juice," Iris said, "I copped this." She pulled a bottle of red wine out from under the car seat.

"What's that for?"

"Well, have you thought about how we're going to get them to drink their own potion? We know they suck down red wine like crazy, so we lace a bottle and you show up at their party with a little present."

"What party?" Megan asked.

"Come on. You think they're going to miss commemorating the anniversary of their death? Get real. They'll be out at the Blue Mesa at dusk; I'd bet my telescope on it."

"But how am I going to persuade them I'm a friendly visitor?" Megan wondered. "They hate me like poison now."

"Only because they think you're an unbeliever. You only have to convince them you've converted."

"I don't know how . . ."

"Oh, come on," Iris said. "Just charm them. They like you. They could have killed you and didn't. You're one of the recruits they really wanted. Just let them think they can have you again."

It was all Megan could do to keep from jumping out of her skin during the time she was home baby-sitting Abe and eating dinner with her parents. She excused herself before dessert, supposedly to go up to her room to study, but actually to sneak out the window and meet Iris.

Of course her father would pick this night to want to go over her math with her, and of course Abe would want her to play Legos with him. She could barely concentrate on either. Living two lives was beginning to take its toll. She'd be glad when tonight was over—whatever its outcome.

"Think I'm going to turn in early," she told her dad. "I'm really beat. If anyone calls, don't wake me up. I'd rather not be disturbed."

Iris had the motor running when Megan dropped from the eave onto the sparse grass of the side yard and hopped into the car. They drove in silence for a while, each absorbed in her own thoughts. When they got to the garage where the bus was parked, Megan jumped out, taking the doctored bottle of wine with her.

Iris stuck her head out the window. "You sure you can handle this by yourself?"

Megan shrugged. "I don't know. Who else is there to do it, though? Funny, I've never thought of myself as a particularly courageous person. But here I am in this weird situation where I have to be courageous because there's no one else to do the job, and it has to be done. I am scared, though."

"I know," Iris said. "I'd come with you if I could. But they'd only be suspicious. I'll be waiting for you in the mountains."

"Okay," Megan said, climbing up into the driver's seat of the bus, pulling the door shut, and revving up the huge, old engine. She pulled it out of the garage and waved out the window at Iris, then headed out of town, toward the desert and the Blue Mesa, feeling more alone than she ever had in her life.

Iris was right; a party was in full swing by the time Megan parked the bus at the edge of the highway. This one looked as though it was strictly Band members. She gathered her courage and brought her wine and tried to put on a face that said "friend."

They were clearly shocked to see her.

"A girl who likes to flirt with danger," James said when Megan walked into the circle of car lights and pushed herself up onto the hood of the Camaro.

"I changed my mind," she said in what she hoped was a tone of totally believable sincerity. "I've had a few days on my own to think and . . . well, I started to really miss you all. It just didn't seem like much of a life around here without you."

"Megan got bored without our thrilling company," Laura said. She looked skeptical, but did come over to where Megan was sitting. She began flicking Megan's dangly earrings with her finger, taunting.

Shane seemed less suspicious. "Maybe she's really come 'round," he said.

"I believe her," someone else said, coming out of the shadows. It was Toby. Megan felt a tumble of emotions rush through her. She was so happy to see him. He'd been avoiding her at school, skipping band practices, but now here he was. Then he came closer and put his arm around her and she could see it wasn't really the Toby she knew. There was something very different about him, something older.

More weary. They'd gotten him, it was clear. Now the question was, could she free him?

She smiled at everybody, hoping no one would notice the tremor in her hand as she offered her bottle of wine.

"I brought a little something for the celebration," she said. "I think it's the kind you like."

Shane took the bottle and was the first to drink from it. "So," he said when he'd taken a long pull on the bottle, then passed it along to James, "you understand why tonight is special?"

"That's why I'm here," she said. "I wanted to share it with you."

"Such a dramatic change of heart," Laura said. Megan could hear the sarcasm in her voice, but she didn't seem suspicious of the wine. At any rate, she took a deep drink from the bottle.

"If she wants back in so bad, why don't we let her prove it?" Natalie said. "Why don't we initiate her tonight?"

Megan shivered. She had to keep this from happening. She hoped the purple liquid would kick in, and fast. She hadn't known how potent it was, so she'd just poured all she'd taken onto the bottle of wine. From the looks of things, she'd mixed up a strong potion. Within a few more minutes, the members of The Band had gone into a kind of slow motion, their speech halting, their conversation not quite tracking. Megan knew this was her moment; she had to move now, or forget the whole thing.

"I have a small surprise," she announced softly when she felt they were ready.

"Yeah?" James said, suspicion underlying the fog in in his voice. "Like what?"

"I want to take you all for a little ride."

"Where?" Joey asked.

"I don't even see a car," Natalie said, looking out into the desert.

"I parked by the highway," Megan said.

"Why should we go for a ride with you?" Laura asked, her words slurring against each other.

"Because I know what you want and I can help you get it," Megan said and looked hard and unflinchingly at all of them.

"What is it we want, Megan?" Shane asked, testing.

"Release," Megan said. "Freedom. And I can get it for you."

"Why should we trust you?" Laura asked.

"Because you don't have any better offers," Megan said, then waited for their reply.

Everyone stood very still. The only sound shimmering through the desert night was the tape in the boom box. Finally Shane told everyone, "All right. Let's see what Megan is offering us."

They all ambled across the darkened desert. When they got to where Megan had parked the bus, they stopped and stood transfixed. They seemed in a trance, even beyond what the purple liquid had done to them. No one said anything cynical or sarcastic or skeptical. They just slowly began following one another, getting on, as though they'd been waiting for precisely this— for their bus to arrive and take them away.

When they were all on board, Megan hopped up into the driver's seat, cranked up the old engine, and began heading across the desert, toward the mountains, through the dead of night. The whole way there was no sound except for the low rumbling of the engine and the James Taylor tape playing on the boom box propped on the backseat. Every once in a while, Megan would look over to where Toby was sitting. He never looked back at her. It was as if she was part of his past. She hoped she would be able to bring him back into their present. But right now she had to keep her mind on driving, had to get to the exact right spot.

As the desert gave way to foothills, and then to high, treacherous mountain roads, she began looking out for the markers she and Iris had made note of. The Shell station on the right. Then around the next curve, a sign for the Mountainview Lodge. She was getting close. And then, there it was—a switchback bend in the road, the sheer drop-off separated from the blacktop by a guard rail. She could see the parking lights of Iris's car up on a dirt road to the right. They blinked twice, their signal. She braked the bus and pulled it off onto the shoulder, then turned so it was pointed toward the guard rail on the other side of the road—pointed toward the abyss.

None of her passengers seemed even to have noticed that they'd stopped. She turned and looked at them one more time, then went down the aisle and took Jenny Gonzales and Toby by the hand. When she had them safely out, she turned them over to Iris, then dashed back into the bus, jumped inside and released the emergency brake, then jumped out. They'd practiced this part so many times she did it in just a few seconds.

From there, things left her control. Other forces seemed to take over. At first the bus didn't move. Megan was afraid it was stuck.

What happened next she would remember as long as she lived. The night sky, which had been filled with stars, suddenly darkened with tumbling clouds. A light rain began misting down, getting heavier until it was a deluge. Then there was a heart-stopping clap of thunder as the sky turned day-white with lightning and the bus began to roll, slowly at first, then picking up speed as it lumbered across the road, over the opposite shoulder, and through the guard rail.

Then, as another burst of lightning lit the sky, the bus arced into midair and hung suspended for a moment as the distant strains of James Taylor singing a plaintive "Fire and Rain" came down from the sky.

And then it was gone—the music and the bus and The Band. Not down the incline into a tumbling, fiery crash, but into someplace beyond midair.

Megan hugged herself and felt a shiver run through her as it disappeared. Like a letter sliding into an envelope that was finally getting sent.

Epilogue

➤

"You vicious superpower!" Toby wailed as Iris took another country from him.

"I am not vicious," Iris defended herself. "I'm just a great Risk player is all. One of my many talents."

"She's a genius," Megan said. "We just all have to recognize it. Give her a medal or something."

"I'm willing to give both of you medals," Toby said, suddenly serious. "You saved me by the skin of my teeth. Jenny, too. I guess she's told you how much she appreciates it." He leaned across the game board and gave Megan a kiss that had more than gratitude in it.

"We saved them, too," Megan said after thinking a moment, not needing to give "them" a name. "Now they're free. Now they don't have to wander restlessly preying on teenagers. Especially cute teenagers like this one." She reached over and ran her hand through Toby's hair.

"Excuse me if I go barf," said Iris. "Are you feeling better, Toby?" she added, truly concerned.

"Every day," he said. "Like I'm coming back from some terrible fever."

132

"With me," Megan said, "it's getting past the dreams. Getting to nights without nightmares."

"Uh, Parental Unit Alert," Iris said in a low voice, signaling the arrival of Megan's dad in the family room. He sat down on the sofa by the gameboard they had spread out on the floor, took off his baseball cap, and said, "Megan, your mother and I have been thinking. You've been grounded for three weeks now, and we've decided to let you off the hook."

"Really?!"

"Yeah. You look so pale and tired. We think maybe it's on account of your not getting out enough lately. Not getting enough stimulation or excitement."

It was all Megan and Iris and Toby could to to keep straight faces while Megan put on her most serious tone and said, "Thanks, Dad. Now that you mention it, it *has* been pretty boring around here."

Megan and her friends had only one more problem: How *were* they going to explain to Uncle Wally what happened to that school bus?

CARMEN ADAMS lives in a remote area on the northern coast of California where she writes, races motorcycles, and trains wolves.

TERRIFYING TALES OF
SPINE-TINGLING SUSPENSE

THE MAN WHO WAS POE Avi
71192-3/$3.99 US/$4.99 Can

DYING TO KNOW Jeff Hammer
76143-2/$3.50 US/$4.50 Can

NIGHT CRIES Barbara Steiner
76990-5/$3.50 US/$4.25 Can

ALONE IN THE HOUSE Edmund Plante
76424-5/$3.50 US/$4.50 Can

ON THE DEVIL'S COURT Carl Deuker
70879-5/$3.50 US/$4.50 Can

CHAIN LETTER Christopher Pike
89968-X/$3.99 US/$4.99 Can

THE EXECUTIONER Jay Bennett
79160-9/$3.99 US/$4.99 Can

SPINE-TINGLING SUSPENSE
FROM AVON FLARE

NICOLE DAVIDSON

THE STALKER	76645-0/ $3.50 US/ $4.50 Can
CRASH COURSE	75964-0/ $3.50 US/ $4.25 Can
WINTERKILL	75965-9/ $3.99 US/ $4.99 Can
DEMON'S BEACH	76644-2/ $3.50 US/ $4.25 Can
FAN MAIL	76995-6/ $3.50 US/ $4.50 Can
SURPRISE PARTY	76996-4/ $3.50 US/ $4.50 Can

AVI

THE MAN WHO WAS POE	71192-3/ $3.99 US/ $4.99 Can
SOMETHING UPSTAIRS	70853-1/ $3.99 US/ $4.99 Can